NOW AND FOREVER

Now &

Forever

A Novel
of Love and Betrayal
Reincarnate

MAX EVANS

UNIVERSITY OF NEW MEXICO PRESS

ALBUQUERQUE

Library of Congress Cataloging-in-Publication Data

Evans, Max, 1925–
    Now and forever : a novel of love and betrayal reincarnate /
Max Evans.— 1st ed.
        p. cm.
    ISBN 0-8263-3318-4 (cloth : alk. paper)
    1. Triangles (Interpersonal relations)—Fiction.
    2. Hallucinations and illusions—Fiction.
    3. Male friendship—Fiction. 4. New Mexico—Fiction.
    5. Betrayal—Fiction. 6. Murder—Fiction. I. Title.
PS3555.V23 N69 2003
    813'.54—dc21
                                    2003010646

Design: Mina Yamashita

Now & Forever

One

There is no way that anyone who had seen Ray Morris and me grow up together, often side by side in the most loyal of fun-loving friendships, could possibly imagine that someday we would want to murder one another—and actually move to do so. Such an emotion is usually enacted by either jealousy, money or . . . a woman, or all three. There was no way I could imagine any one of these severing such a deep friendship, but it happened just the same, in an unimaginable form.

In a way, I suppose, this act had been inevitable ever since we high schooled together in Albuquerque. We had developed the same interests early—girls and rocks. That's right, rocks. The grass-green ones of malachite copper, pearl white crystals of beryllium, the heavy, chocolate-black ones of manganese, the rose quartz of the richest gold deposits held our fascination in an ever-tightening clutch.

We strained to outdo each other in our collecting. Sometimes alone, more often together, roaming the New Mexico deserts and mountains for hours and months searching out the most colorful specimens the earth had so reluctantly offered up from her boiling bowels of magma. Then we began to wonder how and why they had been formed, and the first thing you know we were reading endless volumes on mineralogy, geology, and mining and making excited comparisons with our own actual findings. It became a part of us. The genetic minerals of our blood responded and reached out for the mother minerals of the earth and our intense shared interests bound us together as closely as the most loyal Mafia dons.

The girls, with even more mystery and rarity than the divergent rocks, were just as important to us. We spent an equal time in research with them—the difference being that I seemed to have developed a better knowledge and touch with rocks than my buddy, Ray Morris, while he had the edge on me with the women—not much, but enough. I could never understand it since our looks and builds were average and about equal.

I think maybe he was blessed with a little more conversational ability than I was. There was that indefinable something he projected that had a better draw than mine. It didn't bother me much in those days, however, because there were plenty of girls around. Some people are resentful of second best in the Olympics. Not me. The color silver is in a close contest with turquoise blue as my favorite color.

There was one way Ray and I were very different—I loved exploring the ancient Anasazi Indian ruins for the spiritual mystery they gave me, while Ray was interested only in the mineral formations.

These ruins that were scattered all over central and northern New Mexico. I could spend wondrous hours just walking about among the piles of sandstone rocks that were once the walls of family homes built hundreds, some even thousands, of years, before. These pueblitos enchanted me. I seemed to feel spiritual presences there and felt at home myself. I never told anyone, not even my best friend, but the presence of those *Before People* actually brushed around my neck and tugged at my clothing letting me know that they recognized my knowledge of their presence. It was as certain as the taste of onions or the texture of ice cream. I actually seemed to be able to make out a word now and then. I was amazed that I could understand the ancestral Tewa and Tiwa words. I wondered how it could be. What could it possibly portend? Maybe that I was nuts. Anyway, it was an intimacy of spirit, from an ancient place that I could not bring myself to attempt to share with anyone.

It was an enormous thrill whenever I found a perfect arrowhead or a skinning knife. Soon my collection numbered over a hundred arrowheads, tools—including a stone axe—and scores of potsherds of multiple designs and colors. They were all carefully separated and catalogued according to where they came from. I even had two valuable, fluted Folsom Points. These were the ones used by Folsom Man, whose first home was near the little cinder-mining and cattle town of Folsom, in northeastern New Mexico. The first one of these fluted points was discovered by a black cowboy. It was found buried in the ribs of a rare bison and was determined to be just over eight thousand years old. For a long time archeologists had used this as the discovery point of the first natives of America, and then a few years later a spear point lodged in the chest of an ancient, extinct animal near Clovis, New Mexico, on the far eastern side of the state was found to be several hundred years older than the Folsom Point. The race to find an even earlier inhabitants of the first Americans has been going on ever since.

Ray did show some measured interest in the great malpais bluffs just west of Albuquerque, but while I was photographing the pictographs for spiritual signs and other symbols, he was studying them to see if he could find a denominator for minerals. He never did.

I have to give him credit, though; he showed enormous patience with me on these outings. Besides studying the landscape and the ground underneath for any sign of minerals, he would pass his time hunting for anthills. The size of these anthills was pretty impressive—some were eight feet in diameter and a foot high. He discovered that near pueblitos the ants would occasionally lug a turquoise bead up to the top of their hill.

On one of several trips we took up to the white bluff ruins on the fabled San Cristobal ranch, south of Santa Fe, I came across a bird point—a small arrowhead made to shoot wild birds such as turkey and quail. When I found this flawlessly chipped, white flint bird point with a sharp blood-red tip—made red by nature, not bird blood—I marveled at the skill it had taken to accomplish this tiny, delicate piece of art. I was still fingering my find and appreciating it when my ruminations were shattered by Ray yelling as he came near me.

"T.C., you are not gonna believe what I found!" He half stumbled toward me in his excitement.

His enthusiasm really surprised me because during all our explorations his unparalleled patience with me had hidden this kind of excitement. I looked down at his extended hand and saw three beautiful turquoise beads carefully cradled there.

"These are the most perfect ones I've ever found," he said. "And look at this one. Ain't it a jewel, T.C.? They were all three just stacked up together waiting for me to find them."

"Those are terrific, Ray!"

Two of the beads were small undamaged round

turquoises with a tiny hole in the center, but the third was a teardrop shape the size of an unshelled pecan, with a tiny hole at the narrow end. It was smooth and complete, and the color was beautiful.

"Now tell me this, T.C., just how did a tiny little ant carry this thing up to the top of that hill? Talk about engineering!"

"Or maybe teamwork? It must have taken, what, four or five . . . or ten, to move that?"

"At least that many, maybe more. Think of the difference in size!"

"Wow, what a find! Aren't you glad you tolerate my obsession now?"

"Yeah," he said still admiring his treasures. "What have you found today?"

I almost hesitated to show him my beautiful bird point, but it was too good to keep to myself. "Hey, it's been a bountiful day, my fine friend. Looky here what I got."

He took it carefully and held it up where the bright sun could reveal the details of the small red tip. He studied it with admiration. Then he said, "Man, talk about engineering. That old boy knew how to pinpoint a vein. He would have made a great mining engineer."

That was his ultimate compliment.

Later that night—maybe after midnight—it came to me how the teardrop pendant might have gotten there. I couldn't wait until morning so I picked up the phone and called Ray. He answered half asleep and mumbling.

"Ray, I think I have figured out how the bead, the teardrop bead, got up there." I waited for a response, but got a small groan. "Well, I figure that the bead was already dropped there when the ants started building their hill."

"Aww, go to bed, T.C," and he hung up the phone.

Shortly after I found my treasured bird point, I read an article in *New Mexico Magazine* about how the pot hunters were beginning to destroy the history of our state by picking up artifacts. Removing them was interfering with the archaeologists' ability to trace different Indian tribes and pinpointing the time of each tribe's existence.

But it was even worse than that, I knew. Pot hunting was almost like tearing apart a spirit's soul. This began to really bother me, and finally I reached a point where I could consider parting with my treasured collection. I put my collection into a box, along with all the catalogued information, and an unsigned note explaining that I had read the magazine article and was sorry to admit that I was one of these "pot hunters" and please return these objects to the Indian council and they could decide what to do with them. And please ask the spirits to forgive me.

I called Ray, told him what I was going to do and asked him to drive me to Santa Fe to the museum. I carried the box in my lap all the way. I sweated underneath it and my hands were wet. This was not easy.

I went alone inside the museum, while Ray waited in the car, and found the curator's office. There was a lady with gray hair at the front desk. I placed the box on the desk and left the room without saying anything. I walked out as fast as I could manage without actually running, holding my breath somewhere in my body besides my lungs and expecting to be stabbed right through the heart by a Folsom Point on a long shaft before I could reach Ray's car.

"Let's go."

"Jesus, T.C., you're as pale as a ghost. What happened in there?"

"Don't ask. Just drive." He did.

As Ray silently drove me back to Albuquerque, I felt guilty, but much relieved. About halfway home, I relaxed.

Ray said, "I been hoping we can go down south next weekend and look over the Hillsboro/Kingston mining areas. What do you think? Can you go?"

"Yeah, that sounds great. I think we should do that."

He drove another mile or so without saying a word, then he said, "I kept my beads because the ants had already earned them."

I had no comment on that one. I didn't know it then, but I should have listened more carefully.

It was mostly a happy life, filled full of two major loves. Our parents were modestly wealthy business people—his in the construction business, mine in real estate. They had a hard-work/hard-play ethic that had been seamlessly transferred to Ray and me, especially loyalty to friends, which we knew, should come above all else in life. That had always been the totem of my family. I could always hear my father saying "Son, you'll make a few friends and a love or two that will be more important than family."

I was either at Ray's house or he at mine most of the time. Our folks accepted each of us as their own. I had an older sister in college at UCLA, and his two kid brothers looked up to us as heroes. I never figured that one out. We had played football side by side in high school—Ray as left tackle, me as left guard. We certainly were not outstanding, just competent. We did win second at the state tournament in tennis doubles, however, with our parents right there yelling encouragement as if we were in the national finals. We both had grades ranging from B+ to A- and were assured of our choice of colleges. I suppose from our early interest in rocks it was a natural evolution we both chose the same subject in the same school—the state school of mines in Socorro, New Mexico, a fine little school—highly rated nationally—right in the middle of several small, old mining communities. These afforded easy accessibility for field studies and gave us a big jump up on lots of the students around the world. Another plus: it was a ninety-minute-drive due north to home, making it easy to change over from rocks to girls.

Besides being on a growth boom, Albuquerque was also the home of the state's largest university. Women of our age group were plentiful. It was a fun and experimental, physical time at home and a satisfying study for a successful future at school. All was in order just like the planets. At our age, in those days, the moon was made for songs of love, the blue night light of passion. Only later did we realize it had been pitted and scarred by uncountable comets.

Two

I fell in love. I suppose it happens to everyone, or at least they think so, but at the time I was quite certain that I had a monopoly on the experience. I was sure that among the uncounted millions of people who had inhabited the earth, that I, Thomas Charles Young, was the only one who loved with such passion, such chest-hurting reality, such toe-curling numbness. I knew that anything that intense would surely last through several forevers. Her name was Julie, Julie Goodwin. What a simple and royal name. It belied the complex intellect under her thick reddish brown hair. She was small, almost delicate, but with a suppleness about her body and a look out of her slanted blue-green eyes that added an external strength to her inner core of solidity.

We met at one of those backyard parties that the ambitious seem to always give during the period when they are close to truly getting rich for the first time. The lawn tables were loaded with fresh flowers and delicious food—mostly of the Southwestern variety, tacos, burritos, red and green chile salsa dips and chips. Beverages flowed freely from the two-man bar. The concrete patio served as a dance floor while a local band belted out swing. Periodically, to liven up the crowd, they would blast a rock and roll number.

Julie's father owned a heavy construction firm so it was natural that he and my realtor father were drawn to each other in business and because of this association had become really good friends. Our mothers liked each other, too. They made a pleasant foursome, laughing at jokes that would not have been so funny to the very poor. Most of the guests had this camaraderie of the newly-well-off— inoculated with their mutual success.

Julie and I had been aware of each other, but never had made a social connection. She had just returned to New Mexico from a private Eastern school. At first, her father was dismayed that she had decided not to continue her schooling: then he chose to hire her as an executive secretary in his firm. To his amazement and pride, he discovered that she was a natural on the job: friendly, efficient, totally competent.

I couldn't keep from observing the crowd as I would

an award ceremony or a championship ball game. A few more drinks and the little clustered groups changed members. One could look away for a moment and a new bunch would be formed.

Everyone but the youngsters were working on climbing the proverbial ladder. They laughed, they kidded one another and they were also watching for any opening to better themselves both socially and in business. The most successful at this ancient game also controlled their drinks the best. The skilled name droppers—those who could slip powerful friends slickly into casual conversations—were also the winners. The movement of bodies—carefully groomed and casually dressed—was as planned and obvious as a billboard. Some of the rungs on the ladder were softly stepped on as the climbers reached up for a higher crosspiece, others were being trod upon like bugs, but were unaware because of booze, insecurity or desperation. I don't know how I knew what I was observing before I was out of high school. I had been able to *see* certain things very early, long before my experiences warranted the ability. I was soon to find out, though, that I was blind in certain areas that should have been obvious.

When Julie and I finished our first-ever fast dance together, I was surprised to catch a glimpse of our parents watching us, talking and smiling in what they thought was their hidden appreciation of the two of us together. In actuality, they looked as if they felt totally responsible for our meeting. There are as many and diverse ways of arranging a mating as there are stitches in a circus tent.

A few young guests were splashing in the pool. Their exuberant yells and laughter knocked ragged holes in the air. The drinks were beginning to dominate food so the chatter of both the older and younger people was rapidly growing in volume. The band was feeling the effects of their own visits to the bar during breaks and were settling into some wilder rock and roll. The party was beginning to blast.

Julie and I looked at each other and we both read the message at the same instant. We would grow to treasure this ability to communicate silently. We quietly escaped to the front of the large adobe house. Since her Chevy convertible was parked in a handier spot than my Ford sedan, we jumped in and took off, my heart racing in sync with the motor as if we had escaped being boiled in a great pot of oil. Soon we were unaware of anything but ourselves and what we wished to see and feel.

She looked at me smiling and said, "Let's go to the zoo."

I was pleasantly surprised and said, "Leaving one for the other?"

"Yes, but the animals are better behaved there."

And we laughed together at this silliness—the greatest of all bonds.

There was not an animal, a bird or an imported bush that she did not comment on. Her caring vitality was contagious. As she watched a mountain lion perched up on a pile of rocks that imitated its natural habitat, I saw and felt the awe she had for all these caged animals.

I think she said, 'Look, T.C., how the cougar's tail curls down the rocks to make a perfect design,' but I can't be certain because the southwest sun was causing the streaks of gold in her hair to shimmer reddish-bronze and it did something strange to my brain. I reached over and smoothed my hand down it. She turned to me, looking straight into my eyes and right on through the back of my head and kissed me softly blind. Yes, it really is true. Love strikes one sightless to many things from its very inception.

We started going steady. We were together at every opportunity. We took short trips on weekends up to the art colony of Taos, to the old mining towns of Cerrillos, Madrid, and Golden all within an hour or two from home. We enjoyed the moment—a beer in the old bar in Madrid, a sunset from the top of nearby Sandia Peak and the high desert silences in the vast open spaces surrounding our city. We discussed countless ideas of great wisdom, of course. Soon, we were reading each other's words before they were spoken. An eternal and fatal sign. Besides ancient genes, youth and compatibility caused every touch of a hand, a knee, our lips to become a tingling warmth that was as undeniable as the existence of the sun. It seemed the whole world had turned to high-grade gold. We would be together all our lives, work well, have kids, bury one another. That's the way a zillion songs and dreams go, anyway—and we had already accepted the proverbial dream as an undeniable reality. Youth.

We preferred to be alone, but that's not the way this world works. We double-dated with Ray and his numberless conquests and had a great time no matter who we were with. Even with all the social activities, I managed to keep my grades up. Julie inspired me to even hardier studies. I soon found myself at the head of the class for the first time in my life.

We carefully, exultantly, planned a last weekend trip together before my final exams. I got off at noon on Friday and picked her up in my 1950 Ford sedan in front of her apartment near Old Town. She had packed a small bag. She was the only woman—including all my friends and relatives—who could pack a tiny bag and somehow be perfectly outfitted for any casual occasion. I suppose it had something to do with that same ability she had to expertly organize the people, the papers and the multiple phone calls at her dad's business. Anyway, it was a marvel to me. Our fishing poles were also thrown in—just in case. We had both fished for mountain trout with our families in the cold blue-green streams of Northern New Mexico ever since we could walk. It would be a thoughtless sin to take a trip without packing our fishing gear.

We had both been to Santa Fe and Taos many, many times and we both loved the drive north, but that day was different. The land, the sky, the very air we breathed was special. In that one hour the terrain varied from rolling grasslands of the high desert to malpais mesas created by the ancient lava flows from now inactive volcanoes. We drove between the blue Jemez range to the west, and the mighty Sandias that dominated the city of Albuquerque. Northeast of the San Pedros, the Cerrillos Hills blurred. There the Anasazi had mined the blue-green turquoise even before the Spaniards came and took over the mines. The Anasazi had traded the worshipped gem stones with the Mayas, from far south in Central America, for ceremonial parrot feathers and other rare goods long before the Spanish or Anglos had even seen this land.

We could soon see the adobe houses of Santa Fe embracing the foothills of the Sangre de Cristos, part of the Rocky Mountain range that snakes and thrusts mighty holes in the sky all the way north into Canada.

We checked into La Fonda Hotel on the corner of the historic plaza and had a Mexican beer in the bar and watched the passing people. We decided to have an early dinner at Maria's Mexican Kitchen on Cordova Road.

I ordered chile rellenos, and Julie had cheese enchiladas with red chile sauce. I'm here to tell you that not only did these melt in your mouth, they seemed to melt your entire body. We had margaritas to help soothe the fire, and talked about such a variety of endless things that most of them were forgotten before a new idea came into our heads. There never seemed to be enough time to say all the things that were boiling up inside. Never. I suppose that was just part of young love. Who in all the world has ever explained this exactly?

There was the usual mixture of customers in the place—politicians, tourists, ranchers and now the first influx of amateur uranium prospectors still timid and looking around at a world as foreign to them as the outer reaches of Tibet. They would soon turn the landscape into giant ant hills and Ray and I would join them in their drive for wealth and the most powerful explosive force the world had ever known—well, except maybe jealousy.

The conversation came easy during and after the Margaritas and the fiery food. It was a fine night in Santa Fe and got better.

When we returned to the hotel, a Mexican trio was playing love songs older than Santa Fe—older than speech—so we had a nightcap, danced a few times then went up to bed and held one another very close. We made love. It was slow and very tender. We didn't have to rush. We had an entire lifetime to relish one another's body. Then we slept the spent lovers' sleep of peaceful depth.

The next day the trip on up to Taos was filled with wondrous sights. Our hearts were so full that everything seemed more beautiful than it ever had before. The magic light and clear air of Taos became even more rarefied as we neared the village. We talked about the air—that it's the very reason why artists had come to Taos from all over the world to work there. Many had stayed, lived and died on the earth that absorbed and sometimes reflected the magic light. Yes, the magic light of the Taos Country. It whispered ancient love songs.

We checked into the Taos Inn just north of the plaza on Pueblo road, admiring the two-story lobby with its large Indian fireplace. The owner, Harold Street, a balding, heavy-set man who somehow seemed trim because of his alert enthusiasm, checked us in and eagerly answered our questions about art galleries. Before we could even get our bags to our rooms, he tried to sell us some shiny black pottery made by a San Ildefonso Pueblo Indian woman named Maria, and also some powerful cedar-wood carvings by Patricino Barela that Mr. Street was mistakenly calling "primitive." These religious, symbolic works seemed strikingly modern to me, far ahead of the woodcarver's time. Our time. Julie told Street we would take a better look later.

The Taos Indian with his hair in double braids, who worked there said, "I'm Augustine. I will take care of you," and he smiled all the while. He was just the opposite of the white-man's view of the stoic Indian. He was known at the pueblo as "Smiley." Augustine took our bags to the room and built us a piñon fire in the small corner adobe fireplace. We were not going to stay in the room for now and I felt we were wasting wood, but Julie whispered, "It will be great when we come back to the room. It will take the chill off."

"Oh," I said, as I handed Augustine a bigger tip than I could afford.

It was a wonder to walk around the plaza with a few other tourists, blanketed pueblo people and the local

Hispanics, who totally dominated the county politically. Somehow the spirits of the past—Spanish dons, the mountain men, prospectors, gamblers, adventurers of every hue, seemed to mix with the present. I felt a chill of openness and abandonment. I've heard that certain sections of Paris create this feeling. I decided I would take Julie there someday and find out the truth of it.

We visited shops where we saw silver and turquoise jewelry of every description, blankets, pottery, Kachina dolls, and stylized watercolors of pueblo ceremonies, dancers, medicine men, and horses. I bought Julie a silk-screen print of wildly colorful dancers and Blue Spirit horses with the white tails and manes that fell to the earth done by the great Pottawatomie Indian artist, Woody Crumbo. I planned to give it to her when we got back home.

Everywhere we went, the shop owners or attendants were respectful of Julie's good taste. I loved listening to her every comment. I was pleased and honored to join her world.

We walked across the center path of the plaza with the intention of going to Gallery A on Kit Carson Road a couple of blocks away. I saw the wino just as he saw me. I felt his intensity even as I looked away. He had me pointed just like a bird dog does a pheasant. I knew from past experience there was no escape. These professionals can spot a sucker like me through a granite mountain.

Just as we stepped into the street that circles the plaza, he confronted us, mainly me. To my surprise he was only in his mid-twenties, with nicely balanced features. His jeans and wrinkled shirt were fairly clean. I usually just handed over a dollar and moved on, but his appearance had thrown me for a twist.

Before he could make his pitch I babbled out, "We buried

my dear ole mom last week. She was sideswiped by a bus. Lingered on for days in a pure agony." No reaction. I continued, "My poor daddy is in prison for fraud, and I'm filing for bankruptcy tomorrow." Still no reaction. "And this very morning, some evil son-of-a-bitch poisoned my dog." I said with as much bitter sadness as I could create.

He stood there staring into my very soul for at least a minute, then he calmly reached into his pocket and without hesitation sorted out a dime from a handful of change and with great solemnity handed it to me, turned as smartly as a castle guard and walked away never looking back. Now that's class. I stared after him for an instant knowing I had been had.

I turned to look at Julie a little embarrassed. I had insulted the man's profession.

She said, with as straight a face as she could manage, "T.C. Young, that is the saddest story I ever heard." Then she let go of her penned up laughter with a gush. Finally she managed to continue, "You should have seen your face."

I started laughing, too. At myself, because the wino had really laid one on me. I took her soft, warm hand and we headed, half stumbling, embracing, still in the amusement of the moment, in the direction of the gallery. I wouldn't realize, of course, until later, how precious those seconds of first love would become. I wonder if we are all guilty of overlooking these early, priceless moments. I surely was back then.

After several significant hours, we finally arrived at Gallery A—a new establishment. Mary Sanchez, the director, expertly put us at ease, and gave us all the time we wished to browse without pressure.

Julie and I simultaneously fell in love with a small

Dasburg watercolor of a southern suburb of Taos, simply titled "Talpa." She bought it. It was pretty expensive, but I kept forgetting that she was an executive secretary of a highly profitable firm that was in truth partly her own.

The day slipped away. Dinner time arrived. This time, instead of Mexican food, we ordered lamb chops. We had a grand time listening to a truly great guitarist, Ramón Hernández. The long, narrow room made for a place of intimacy and a feeling of comradeship no matter who sat at the adjoining table—local, national or foreign. The uranium prospectors were here as well—somehow managing to seem out-of-place and then, after a few drinks, comfortable.

After one set of Ramón's music, from the Spanish flamenco to an old Mexican love song, the entire place gave the guitarist a standing ovation.

I said appreciatively to Julie, "That man is a roomful."

She answered, enigmatically, "We seldom see what we have seen."

She paused and turned loose that ever-so-slightly sideways smile, looking up at me with angled eyes of singular poignancy and added, "But we always know when we've really heard beauty with passion."

I answered without thought, "Ramon has shopped his soul in many pretty places." He had somehow touched all here. That must reveal at least a tiny bit of greatness, but of course, I was prejudiced in favor of everything that special night with my Julie.

I felt such a warmth and tingling comfort that night in the blue-smoked bar filled with laughter and the exact right music that I saw everything in a haze of rapture. That's the way it was. The desert. The mountains. The art. The music. Taos. Julie.

Three

It was Julie, who said, "What a morning, T.C." She was looking out the window. "Just come over here and take a look. Did you ever in your entire life see a more perfect morning than this to go fishing? Let's go up to Twinning. You want to?"

I didn't have to go to the window to make up my mind. I said, "You bet."

"You know, that is my favorite little fishing place in the whole world. My folks and I have been going up there since I was a teeny little girl." She smiled, tilting her head and mouth in that way that would make a rodeo bull chase his tail like a puppy, and continued, "Get ready. Time's a' wastin'."

The road to the village of Arroyo Seco was paved nearly to the mouth of the canyon where Twinning Creek murmured in unknown tongues on its way to the Rio Grande. I stopped the car and pulled to the side at the top of the hill just before we headed down into the canyon. We looked back at the tiny Spanish village of Arroya Hondo. It was a valley both flattened and rounded with small, green checkerboard fields of alfalfa, corn and grassy pastures where a few cows and horses grazed. It looked like a perfect abstract painting.

"I always get a strange kind of thrill right here—on this spot—for some reason." Julie said. "It's as if . . . well, I feel like there are special spirits that are overseeing this valley . . . this village."

"Me, too. That's why I stopped." I started the car and said, "But, we better get going," as I pulled back onto the graveled dirt road to Twinning Canyon. The canyon was narrow with heavy vegetation, spruce, pine, and oak brush protectively covered the steep walls of the mountains on both sides. Now and then tiny, intensely green, meadows allowed us glimpses of our favorite stream below the road. Soon the white, black spotted trunks of the aspen trees intermingled with the dark green and blue forest to give distinctive relief.

We approached a small grassy spot where I could easily park. I asked her, "Is this good enough? Or do you think we'd have better luck farther up?"

"Oh, here, T.C. Right here. I'm too anxious to wait another second." She was already gathering up her gear.

"You know that they are talking about building a ski resort at the head of the canyon?"

"Yes," she answered, "my dad said something about it. I think I hate that . . . I mean really hate that. Don't you?"

"Yeah. A few years back, we could come up here and there wouldn't be more than three or four cars in the whole canyon all day, and today we have already seen six or seven."

"Eight." She corrected. "But we've only seen one fisherman."

We were quiet for a moment, just looking at each other. I was thinking about what was, what is and what is bound to be. I wondered what *she* was really thinking. I suddenly felt that this might be the last time we would ever have such solitude to fish and absorb this unique world around us that we both selfishly felt was ours alone. I didn't say anything else. I didn't want to risk spoiling the mood of the present.

The air was so pure and sweet it could have been bottled and sold for champagne of oxygen. We unloaded our gear. Julie had had the good sense to order take-out breakfast—fried egg sandwiches, two small cans of pork and beans, two apples and a jug of water. We picked out a couple of big rocks to sit on while I ate so much, I was pleasantly numb.

Then the challenge, the mystery of the circling, dark water in the nearest hole, overcame the lilting beauty of the total stream as I slipped quietly up on it, moving as near to the motion of a stalking cat as I could and eased the two, wormed hooks into the water. I forgot everything, every problem that had ever been or could possibly ever be in anticipation of the fishes' feeding. That's what the Great Mystery surely had in mind when he conjured up the sport—no, the life—of fishing in a pure mountain stream. Time was no more. The eternally splendid vacuum enveloped all. Nothingness and the infinite prevailed.

Then the tiny tug. The pull. The miss.

One worm was gone. Shakily, hastily, I replaced it and eased the two hooks back into the water. I knew I'd get him next time. Ah, the slippery game-player returned. The tug. The pull. The solid weight after my flipping motion gave the signal that I had it hooked solid. I swung up and to the side to miss the bushes and the trees behind me. The glistening twelve-inch rainbow flopped in the grass with all the colors of Renoir's pallet flickering damply from its sides. Fulfillment beyond any earthly reason flowed in my blood. The first catch is meant to be the best so we will be enticed into seeking its repetition. Shooting dice with the water gods.

I caught two more out of that hole before moving on. I finally had four keepers from ten to twelve inches. The others I had carefully unhooked and slipped back into their perpetually moving home.

Satisfied, I sat down on a cut bank and looked down stream for Julie. There she was, moving steadily, fly-fishing, walking in her sneakers, jeans rolled up, but wet almost to her waist, up the middle of the stream. The fly line turned golden wet as it rolled back and forth, back and forth, as she drew moving pictures in the sky. The droplets from the flying line became minute jewels as they perpetually returned to the stream in a hypnotic rhythm as old as love making.

The beauty of the surroundings and the creek, and the woman I adored moving up the middle of it was about all my eyes could take and deliver to my heart. She had a grace in her careful steps that seemed to sense the underwater terrain and rocks so that she never stumbled. She just moved like a symphony conducted by a director that only she could see.

It was a useless waste of the spirit to have any more doubts. There she was. Right out there, encompassing my vision, fusing my soul with hers. It was a profound relief to know and admit that she was all there was for me. Julie. My Julie.

The sun glanced off her hair in a crimson aura waving, undulating as the flesh of her body moved in harmony with the stream. She stopped and moved to the edge of a wide riffle casting her fly line and its hook in perfect rhythm. That special attunement was recognized by a ten-inch trout. It rose and tried to swallow the Cadis fly. It did. Julie moved sideways reeling in until the fish flopped wildly in the shallows.

I was, of course, mesmerized. Then I yelled. "Hey, save some for me." She looked up from the bank where she had unhooked the lovely one. There came that smile shooting inside me deeper than any fish hook ever swallowed.

We had seven fish altogether. We lay on the grass side by side our eyes closed. The mountain sun mingling with the cool air was hypnotizing. Languorous. I napped. Then I awoke. Julie was sitting up, leaning over her bent knees, just looking at me. I felt naked. We soon were.

That night we asked the hotel chef to cook our trout. All seven! Julie invited a couple of tourists from Ada, Oklahoma to join us in our feast. They did, and ordered a bottle of white wine to accompany our meal. It was fun. It was love. It was *our* Taos for this one night.

How, oh how, could a heart so full of love later lust uncontrollably for blood because of the beauty of these moments. All that horror was unseen and far away in the magic of the shortest night there ever was.

Four

Right after a breakfast of fine huevos rancheros (eggs with red chile heated in the delicious fires of hell), we were off in the Ford to explore across the Rio Grande Gorge's western side—an immense piece of dusty blue-green sagebrush desert.

We drove north on the Questa Highway, then turned west toward the Rio Grande gorge on a snaking dirt, partly graveled road. One of my professors at school had given the description of the western side of the momentous gorge as, "You can see all the world that matters." He had prospected for the non-mineral filtering, insulating material of perlite out there and had enjoyed the experience enough to insist I go. Now Julie and I were on our way.

We slowly curved down the gravel road to the John Dunn Bridge. It was amazing to me how Dunn's old toll bridge was in such sturdy shape. The old gambler, stagecoach line owner and all around entrepreneur had done things to last. We ascended on the west side of the Rio Grande along the road that had been so steep that Long John Dunn had dragged a heavy log behind his stagecoach to help keep it from running away on the downhill trip. We topped out. The earth and the sky suddenly appeared to have doubled in size. We soon spotted the wagon-trail jeep road that turned off into the sagebrush to the northwest. It wasn't fit for Ford sedans and I had to drive on top the ruts the best I could to keep from hitting high center. It was a gut jarring ride. Julie was bracing herself with one hand on the dash and the other on the edge of the seat.

I said, "Wanna turn around while we can?"

"Of course not," she answered.

I felt ridiculous for having asked.

After what seemed like a year of bouncing my teeth loose in my mouth, we spotted the fence line where the road turned back east and down to the rim of the great gash in the earth. The road was used just enough to keep it from growing over in sagebrush, but it was smoother.

We could only drive to within a hundred yards or so of the edge, but as rough as the scattered rocks were, we had a reasonably easy time walking to the drop off. I took Julie's hand and guided her to sit beside me and look down into the six-hundred-foot-deep gorge. It was a thrilling shock. Neither of us were prepared for the unprecedented views.

The Rio Grande was in shadow, but even so, it looked like a silver-blue snake oscillating its way to encircle the world. It felt that big. Without question, it must have taken at least a hundred million years for the river to cut its path so deep through the iron hard malpais of volcanic flow.

We were both over awed as we looked up and down the notable laceration until it curved out of sight. I put my arm around her shoulders and she eased one around my waist. We pulled one another closer as our eyes swept across the rippling sagebrush clothed earth and up, up to the magic Taos Mountain, then on past, to Wheeler Peak —the highest point in New Mexico. The remaining, sharp-edged forms of snow on its top appeared that a giant had made a few mighty slashes with a brush of white paint and moved on. The utter massiveness of the rises and drops and space all around and above us was so profound in its silence and encompassing peace that we had no need for speech.

The late sunlight that had been warming our backs dropped leaving the two of us in shadow. The last rays caught on the Sangre de Cristos (Blood of Christ) Range turning the mountains a rosy color, then moved up setting the edge of a few elongated clouds afire. For a few moments the beams jumped from one tip of a peak to another in a reddish orange. It was more beauty than one could assimilate. The great, ageless gash of the river made one's life seem far less than the opening of an eyelid. The earth bulged so hugely that a germ was a giant compared to us.

As the evening chill moved in, I pulled Julie very close to me. We sat still, my arm about her shoulders, hers around my waist, in the ever expanding silence of the vast desert. We got up and walked slowly, with regret, towards the car before the darkness overtook the dim trail. The moment was a special speck in time, but the spreading darkness would soon seem forever.

Five

The next morning we headed home and back to reality—my schooling, her job. We talked about all the things we had done and things we were going to do, then fell silent for several miles. Each in our own world. One thing I knew for sure: I wanted to spend the rest of my life with this girl. I loved everything about her. When we were apart, even a few minutes, she was the one on my mind. My head was full of her. My heart was full of her.

I drove up in front of her apartment. We gathered her belongings. I reached in the back seat to get the Crumbo silk screen print I had bought and handed it to her, "I really got this for you."

She was truly surprised and said, "I did the exact same thing. Can you believe this? The Dasburg is for you. I wanted you to take something back to school that reminded you of me—and our time in Taos."

"I will never need reminders of that, but thank you. It is very special."

We gave each other a thank-you-kiss, then a goodnight kiss. It was hard to leave her. We kept thinking of new things to say so we didn't have to part.

"I'll try to make it home next weekend so we can catch that movie, *The African Queen*, you've been dying to see," I told her as I finally got back into the car.

"Oh, I hope we can. Bogart and Hepburn. I just *love* those two people. I'm pretty sure this is the last weekend it's showing here. I sure hope we don't miss it."

Then we both became redundant, and when she repeated how she loved Bogart and Hepburn, we shared a knowing chuckle and agreed to part.

"We'll work it out. I promise." I knew it was the weekend before finals, and I should be studying, but I could not disappoint her. We threw each other a final kiss and I drove back to school so I could get to an early class the next morning.

Six

I had convinced myself that I could squeeze in another weekend with Julie, but by mid-week I was falling far short of my goals. It was pure torment to think I might miss that special movie with her, but I knew I could not leave school. Besides studying for finals, I had a major paper to complete about the occurrence of manganese in the foothills just behind our school. The paper would determine my total grade average, and I sure didn't want to mess that up at this late date. I hadn't realized how much concentration and time it would require.

As the weekend approached, I told Ray, "I promised Julie that I would take her to see *The African Queen* and now there is no way I can leave here."

Ray said, "While you were in Taos, I got caught up. I'm going home for the weekend. Why don't I take her for you? It wouldn't be any problem at all. Julie's a great gal."

I looked around at the piles of school work and saw I really had no other choice. "I guess that's the next best thing." So, all arrangements were made.

It was the first weekend in months that I was alone.

Besides all the studying, it gave me time to think about my future—about our future, Julie and me. Since I was graduating at the head of my class, I had already received a number of job offers from major mining companies. The boom in uranium had just been launched by the discovery of rich ore deposits in Utah by another engineer named Charley Steen. The pay was inviting. I had considered, or planned, that Julie and I should be married as soon as my job was secured.

I finished my paper Sunday night and I decided to read a book of fiction to relax. At the time I was reading two authors: Jack London and James M. Cain. Both great escapism. I thought about Julie. Her two favorite authors, Colette and Chekhov, spread a little farther.

I fell asleep in the middle of one of Cain's exciting chapters. Now *that* is tired. I had gone to bed with a feeling of almost complete happiness. It was the last time I would ever get that near to man's ultimate dream again. There would be fleeting moments afterwards, but it would never be the same.

Seven

Ray awakened me when he came in about five on Monday morning. He had evidently been up all night drinking beer, among other things.

"Hi, T.C., how'd the paper go?" He seemed totally jubilant. This was odd for so early in the morning. I thought at first he might be drunk, but he seemed to have handled it well.

I answered, "Hey, it went fine. I'm all finished."

"Good," he said. Then he went on, "T.C., you greedy

rascal no wonder you've been keeping that little Julie all to yourself. That's the best lay I've had in a year."

He said it just like that, as if it did not matter. He was paying no more attention than if he had told me he had bought a pair of new socks. It took a moment for the unbelievable truth—the shock—to register. It had only been a week since Julie and I had felt so strongly we would always be together that words were superfluous.

"You dirty son of a bitch," I yelled as I leaped from the bed and went for Ray's throat.

He jumped across the bed and stood with his arms forward to push me away, saying, "T.C., T.C., what in the hell is the matter with you? Have you gone crazy?

"My best friend! You bastard, you're my best friend! How could you do such a terrible thing?" I screamed trying to reach him for the kill, but instead, I tripped over a stack of textbooks whamming my head against the floor.

"What? What? What? Are you angry about me and Julie? I offered to help out. You agreed. It was your idea. Remember?" His voice changed to disbelief. "Hey, are you serious about her? Well, if you are," he said, with what seemed sincerity, "you better be damn glad you found out about her now. Hell, T.C., half the town had rolled her before us."

The adrenaline of my fury had surged so totally and dropped so hard—along with the brain-numbing fall—that my mind quit working before my body did. It was enough time for Ray's smooth voice to take full advantage. He soon had me convinced there might be truth in his words, and somehow before I could think it out, I was about to forgive him.

I found myself saying, "Ray, if you ever see a mosquito biting a friend . . ."

"Yeah?"

"Well, it's not nice to remove it with a double-barreled shotgun blast."

He just stared at me as if he hadn't heard.

Slowly at first, then with an extraordinary surge of disbelief, the horror and pain of such a deceit filled my brain with hot adrenaline. I charged Ray intending to tear his larynx out of his throat and shove it up his ass to the elbow. My hand slipped off his throat with little damage, but I managed to land a hard right alongside his left ear. It spun him around and I never had a qualm about hitting him as hard as I could in the back of his short neck. I had hoped to see his head ripped off and go crashing through the apartment wall like a Civil War cannon ball. It was knocked to the wall, but to my extreme disappointment and suddenly painful sorrow, the body was still attached to it.

Even though we were approximately the same weight and size, Ray had the powerful forearms of a professional lumberjack. Many times in our high school football days, he had used those arms to slap senseless an opposing lineman who dared to bounce me around. I had appreciated it then, but now as he whirled and slapped me crashing over my study table with the inside of my head whirling dizzily around like an egg beater, I no longer had the same appreciation for his once saving and powerful grace.

He stood there staring at me yelling things like: "You stupid son of a bitch. You chicken shit asshole. Have you gone nuts? I save you from a short life of misery, unholy and very expensive hell with a woman known as round heels . . . and . . . and . . . you show your appreciation by trying to tear my goddamned head off."

I was up on my feet by that time. I was waiting for the

scrambled eggs I had for brains to settle a bit. I said, "I hear you, you lying bastard."

"Well then, show your good sense and your honor for our lifetime friendship by apologizing."

It was the gall of his asking me for an apology that did it. I knew I could no longer contest those forearms. This time, as I launched my assault, I aimed the top of my head at the middle of his stomach fully believing I would come out his other side with his backbone hanging around my ears. It halfway worked. I felt that my own ears were ready to break through the skin of his stomach when he let out a lot of noisy air, turned to the side and slapped me across the back of the head. I was on my way past him from my own momentum anyway, but his blow speeded things up considerably. When I butted the edge of the wooden bookshelf with growing force it was just like my uncle Josh said when he fell off a wagon load of hay, "The wind blew, the shit flew and I couldn't see nothing for a day or two."

It took longer than that for me. I saw his blurred face above me, speaking from an undulating mouth.

"What in the hell got into you, T.C.? You gone plumb nuts? Huh? Speak up. Say something. Remember how we used to laugh when we first heard about . . . hell, you know as well as I do . . . an erection has no conscience and damn little judgment."

Then Ray's voice began to fade. The last thing I heard him saying, "What in the world has gone wrong with you attacking a friend over nothing?"

The world? The world was now as dark as the inside of a slab of slate. And then even that was gone.

I was to learn, a little scrape at a time, that it took longer than that for me. It seems that Ray had somehow carried, dragged or in some manner got me to his car and hauled me to the local hospital; where they stopped the flow of blood enough to take fourteen stitches in the top of my head after shaving it like cutting a swath of alfalfa hay. Then, because I remained unconscious from the concussion, I was swiftly moved by ambulance to St. Joseph's in Albuquerque.

I did become conscious in little patches of light and sound. Out of these noises and sights, I slowly got a linear viewpoint of the happenings. Ray had convinced everyone that we were taking a nighttime stroll to relax from our dedicated studies. We had been, without known reason, attacked by a carload of loonies armed with knives and sticks. We had fought with such desperate bravery that they had finally retreated to their automobile and sped away in cowardly retreat. Ray convinced everyone that the Socorro sheriff's department was getting close to the arrest of the dangerous culprits.

My parents came to visit several times a day. After sadly trying to get me to communicate and failing, had kissed me gently and softly assured me I'd be all right soon.

I screamed as loudly as I could, that I was doing just fine all the way round until my best friend had screwed the love of my life and almost knocked my brains out. Evidently no sound exuded from my mouth, for their faces emanated the same pitying looks. Then I watched numbly as my father and mother embraced Ray and thanked him profusely for saving my life and reiterated how lucky I was to have a friend like him. How lucky we all were. How much we all owed him.

Then I saw little snippets of Julie's anxious face above me and knew she was caressing my cheeks and holding my hands for long periods of time. Once I saw through a little hole of light, Julie enter the hospital room, but as soon as she spotted Ray, she whirled and left. He yelled something after her as she exited that I could not understand—and she never came back. I missed her beyond words, even though I had none.

The inside of my head was several miles deep and even wider part of the time, and the pain would run down in red and white streaks to the center, then radiate back and bounce around and scorch my inner skull. I screamed and screamed, but no one heard me—or maybe they were simply ignoring me.

I overheard three doctors in consultation about surgery for a clot, but one said it was dissolving on its own and he was against it. He won. I won, because all of a sudden I knew people again. I could hear my own voice and make it say what I wanted it to. When I spoke, their eyes told me they heard.

Ray had already spent a lot of time alone with me and though I could not answer, I got to where I could understand his meaning. He had told me over and over and over how sorry he was about our misunderstanding, but he was too good a friend for too long a time to tell me anything but the truth no matter how much it hurt my feelings. "For that matter," he said, "It took a lot out of me and I was so hurt I can barely stand up under it even now." He begged me to do just one thing for him. Think of time. The years of time we had spent together against the minutes with Julie. I didn't want to, but I did. I didn't have a hell of a lot else to do at the moment, anyway. I had to admit I could never remember him lying to me . . . certainly not that I was ever aware of. He had always stuck by me with dead-on loyalty in any kind of physical or emotional difficulty I ever had. Then add to these the fact our parents were close and now mine felt deep indebtedness to him for looking after me with such care. Shit!

And now that I was able to communicate, there was no Julie to confront. Why? Why had she deserted me when I was at my most helpless. Why?

I got well to the point I was released from the hospital with a warning to take it easy for awhile. In fact, except for short spells of violent headaches and dizziness every month or so I was just as fit as ever. However, I could not, no matter how I strained, get all the happenings in line. There were the confused bouts of visions and hearings while in recovery that were as scattered as shotguns blasting away at fast flying doves. Sounds came loudly, vanishing to softness, then silence. Bright visions and spots of images moved away as if I stared through the wrong end of a telescope and were reduced so small they finally became nothing but darkness.

For awhile afterward, I even felt indebted to Ray for saving me from what could have truly been a lifetime of misery. I know one thing, the shock of suddenly-shattered, honest love is greater than any sword to the heart or a bookshelf to the brain. If love is indeed blind, then what about friendship? I would later ask myself this question uncountable times.

Since Ray and I were born a day apart, everyone said we could have been twins. We had always been best friends, almost inseparable. He had never lied to me, nor I to him. I kept repeating all these things to myself. The natural trust that evolved through the closeness of our families and our own natural companionship made deceit unthinkable. I finally believed everything he told me. Maybe I was lying to myself, hiding a truth too horrible to accept, making myself blind to spotlights of revelation. But as addled as my reasoning processes were, they added up all those years—a lifetime of them—just as Ray suggested and the odds scaled heavily in his favor. Preponderantly so.

Julie called. The instant I heard her voice I slammed down the receiver. She called three times. Each time I repeated my infantile action. She didn't call again. God!

Eight

Finals were over and I was back home. I told my parents if Julie called to tell her I was out-of-state, but she didn't call. I did, however, receive three letters on her unmistakable embossed, pink stationery. God, how I wanted to read them, but instead, I tortured myself by keeping them around for several days, hugging them to my heart, touching them to my face and breathing deeply for the slightest scent of her perfume. When I couldn't stand the hurt any longer, I burned each one with a kitchen match. I held the last one until the flames touched my fingers, hating to let go.

I tried to hide from everyone, especially Ray. The numbing pain inside me was a living entity within itself. I felt it was miles in circumference and would most certainly stop the beating of my heart and the breathing of my lungs. It was an immense struggle to hide this suffocating agony.

I overheard my dad say, "I hope those kids patch up whatever misunderstanding they had before it's too late. Youngsters are pretty impulsive, you know."

Mother answered, "Oh, I don't think we have to worry about the kids, dear. Everyone knows those two were just made for each other. It's only a silly little lovers' quarrel. We've all had them. They'll soon fix it."

My father was not quite as sanguine, as he answered, "I sure hope so."

How many millions of times had the essence of those same words been uttered before by other people, I wondered. No one could possibly know my feelings of betrayal—feelings that had totally numbed my senses. I was almost incapable of dealing with them.

At the moment I would truly, gladly, have given up ten years of my life for my mother's words to come true. But she was wrong. The grinding pain of jealousy was now too deep to cure.

I was so grateful for school and the excuse of studying—or at least, pretending to study. It gave me time to be alone and sort through my feelings. I had to numb the hurt and enhance the thrill of the unknown future Ray and I were about to launch—the new life of exploration we both had planned for and believed in. Our entire reasoning lives had been spent in one way or another preparing ourselves for this special time. Nothing must stop us now that our timing was so perfect and we were so ready, so anxious.

Ray and I picked up our sheepskins and accepted employment at the same firm—Arondo Mining. We moved to Grants, about sixty miles west of Albuquerque on Route 66, and went to work developing the world's largest uranium reserves. Prospectors from all over America got the oldest kind of greed. They spotted the hills everywhere with their little Geiger counters and ancient hopes. The big mining companies leased, mapped and started drilling programs to block out the ore. It was an exciting and fabulous time—comparable to the California Gold Rush days, but there was so much more at stake—the survival of the world, to be exact—or so we were indoctrinated daily and hourly by all our government reports to the world press.

Booms! Boom towns or boom regions or boom nations, what a ripping time they are. The uranium boom raced to the West out of Washington D.C. and Moscow, Russia. The great nuclear arms race was on. The world was excited, scared and screwy. More of the latter. We were told by the press, the prospectors' rumors, and the grapevine of greed, that uranium in great quantities must be found and mined and turned into protective bombs or we would be blown away to invisible particles by the Soviets. Most Americans—and the rest of the world— certainly believed it.

The professional prospectors of the West turned away from seeking gold, copper, silver and all the other enticing extractive riches from the earth, and traded their burros in for Jeeps and Geiger counters (a small, sensitive, hand-held machine that could crackle out the radio-active presence of the precious and deadly uranium ore). Most of those who came were total amateurs. Their knowledge of geology or prospecting was minimal. They figured it was their chance to get rich quick and they were here to cash in on the boom. This ancient fever—permanently fused in the blood—would surface again and again like untreated malaria, as if it were brand new.

Oh, what a time it was. There were, gas station operators, deputy sheriffs, dry goods and shoe salesmen, accountants, nightclub owners, farmers, barbers, doctorates and illiterates. They came from every state in the Union but the greatest numbers came from Texas, Kansas, and Oklahoma. They all came in search of a big uranium find—and the wealth they were sure came with it. Everyone was trying to find another Ambrosia Lakes deposit (the world's largest body of uranium ore being mined), which was north of Grants, New Mexico, and west of Mount Wilson.

They left their businesses, their families and even their sanity to come West seeking adventure. They covered Utah, New Mexico, Colorado and Arizona as if these states were massive, uneven anthills and some spread out to Idaho, Nevada and California. Moving about in Jeeps and pickups until they could go no further, then on foot, carrying the little black boxes of high expectation, listening raptly for the buzzing crackle that was like bacon frying at warp speed.

Many brought their families to raucous ruin without ever getting a rock worth assaying. Thousand of others found small amounts of infested rock and staked claims expecting to cash in the millions.

At night, the motels of the West were rented and the restaurants were full. But it was in the bars that a great portion of their resources were joyfully, almost desperately, expended along with their conversational dreams. They were reliving the fabled, often phony Wild West of their movie and pulp magazines dreams. Ray and I were not immune to the excitement, but ours was tempered by training and a solid plan for the future.

Some of the poorest counties of the West profited in another unexpected manner. Each and everyone of the claims filed had to be registered and recorded at the county courthouse. It was a windfall of unexpected and often uncounted millions of dollars. It was a time of big thoughts, actions of mostly foolish bravado, and the electricity of expectations. It was a time that was purely American. Risk it all for God, family, country and the Atomic Energy Commission.

Most of the free-lance ore deposits of any quality and quantity were found by maverick geologists who took them straight to their colleagues at big companies and sold—or took stock for—their discoveries. Soon the limited number of uranium mills controlled the entire boom. If a prospector made a discovery, the powers could sweat him down to a small price or tell him to mill his own which of course, with the endless government and financial restrictions, was impossible.

A very few, such as Charlie Steen of Moab, Utah, made it big, while most lost it just as fast as playing at a crooked crap table. A few hundred others made a good business of selling, as soon as possible, any claims that caused the little black boxes to giggle.

The few companies that had the most ore were also in Moab, Utah, and Durango, Colorado, but the world's uranium headquarters was where we were, Grants, New Mexico. At Grants, the Laguna pueblo people and the Navajos had lots of employment at the mines and mills. They were paid wages and some royalties, along with new and drastic changes in their lives that would affect them for generations both very good and very badly.

The town of Gallup—a one-hour drive west of Grants—also shared in the grand adventure. I had heard so many stories about Navajo Paddy Martínez's uranium find that it had become legend to all of us rock hounds.

Paddy was doing all right on his own with a fine wife named Flora, over one thousand sheep, and nine children to help tend them. He was also a sought-after medicine man. His business friends in Grants and Gallup had told him to keep on the lookout for any yellow carnotite rocks.

I heard hundreds of times how Paddy had gone into town to get some baking soda. However, that nearly empty bottle of whiskey found in his pocket after he woke up from a nap on the way home made more sense to me. At any rate, he sat up, casually looking around as he got his bearings, spotted the history-making, yellow tinged rock. It was carnotite. He had found it on Section 19 owned by the Santa Fe Railway. Both Paddy and Section 19 would become famous in all mining circles—Paddy for his discovery of the first of America's most crucial ore deposit, and Section 19 for its massive production of the same. He was awarded a small pension by the company. Ironically to me and many others, Paddy didn't need it nearly as much as the preponderance of the very poor Navajos. He became an extremely popular man not only because he was famous, but because a lot of his Indian friends got their very first well-paying job, ever, mining Section 19.

Paddy Martinez of the Navajo Nation near Gallup and Charlie Steen of Moab, Utah, were neck and neck in leading the thousands of permanent and temporary legends. Some were truth. Some were simple rumors. Yeah, it was a legendary time all right and Ray and I were working smack in the middle of it, learning, earning straight contract salaries all to benefit our future enlarged company.

Nine

Multiple madness always becomes a contagious disease. My own singular, or at the most double, madness concerning Julie and my partner Ray, might have been dwelt up on until I, too, went as berserk as the golden ore chasers. However, what saved me for now was the lack of a place to escape *their* madness. I couldn't take to the hills for they covered them like flies on day-old dung. I couldn't escape in a bar because they were bulging out the doors. The coffee shops and other stores buzzed like working sawmills with talk, talk, talk of the most powerful force ever advanced by man—nuclear energy and the ore it takes to make it work.

As I mentioned before, there were pegmatite veins and dikes thinly scattered across the Rocky Mountain states that caused mountains of money to change hands. These whitish injections of magna into the crevices of the earth cooled eventually forming many small particles of minerals. Their main makeup was feldspar and quartz but most of them had some beryl often crystallized into hexagonal chunks, mica lepidolite (lithium) among many other specimens.

The two minerals that were speckled and sprinkled sparsely throughout the dikes—that fooled so many—were columbite and tantalite. They were mostly in dark peanut-sized metallic particles and widely scattered. But they did have uranium along with their deposits of other rare earth that would cause a Geiger counter to sing a falsetto song of wealth. Many who staked claims and blasted into these dikes were terribly disappointed at the final quantitative assays. Others caught on and sold them as fast as they could after staking their claims without spending a single cent on blasting or assays. These few may have been amateurs at minerals, but they were the wise ones at business. The cash was delivered into their hands by naiveté or greed.

At the beginning of all booms, there are more buyers than sellers. Then the reverse occurs. However, before the plural frenzy subsided, there was the top of the line con, to feast on the demented weakness of greed. A penny stock market sprang up in Denver, Salt Lake City, and our own hometown. Oh, how good it sounded—from a penny to a nickel in one day was a gain of five hundred percent. Often this happened overnight. Sometimes it was even more grandiose when a penny stock reached a dollar—an unthinkable gain. When a few stocks went from a dollar to three or more, just imagine what those sky-stretching yields meant to a human weakness so old the beginning is forgotten. The whole concept of "something for nothing" has ruined more humans lives than smoking, drinking, doping, war, sloth, and card playing combined. Rumors were as wild and frequent as tennis balls at Wimbledon and even harder to pin down.

Penny. Penny stocks. It was the *penny* that seemed like nothing, so people felt like they were getting a free ride and that is why they fed on rumors like vultures on a sun-ripened carcass. Americans feel the penny is so small they resent carrying them in their pockets or purses. Half the closets in the nation contain cans or jars running over with the unappreciated penny. Rarely does one think about a million pennies being ten thousand dollars.

A few stock traders made good money before the Security Exchange Commission shut them down. A few made millions of dollars from nothing but rumors, and often retired South—far South. A tiny few were honest and it was never known how they and their investors came out.

Considering all that would happen shortly, I almost forgot one other great governmental mistake that led to a short-lived, unexpected bonanza for those who read it right. The government agencies that controlled the testing of nuclear weapons, were under great pressure to stay ahead of the Russians. It was the worldwide fear of "The War of Oblivion" that drove them to excess. So, amidst the vicious protests of the few and the deliberate disregard by the masses, they proceeded testing with atomic explosions in the Nevada desert.

People living in the uranium boom area were told that the winds had carried, and harmlessly dissipated, any possible nuclear fallout far to the Northeast. It was not true. Many prospectors in Southern Colorado and Northern New Mexico were suddenly surprised to find radioactivity across land that had previously tested negative. Much time, and a lot of hard-earned—even borrowed—money was spent on worthless claims. The reason: mountain showers had pushed the x-ray material to the earth and washed the deadly substance into natural traps of leaves and twigs where the concentration caused the little black box to announce its rasping discovery. It was all surface material. Worthless. And no one will ever know of the spiritual and physical damage it caused to the myriad inhabitants of the vast plateaus and prairies by these cold blooded and calculated lies. I know this much: The Atomic Energy Commission is never going to tell, even if by some unexpected miracle there was the slightest paper trail left undestroyed.

Ray and I were offered every kind of bribe in the book

by people who believed our paid-for knowledge could short cut their way to the notoriety of a fast fortune. I suppose we were tempted a time or two, but nevertheless we shunted aside all teasing, easy-come thoughts and kept aiming down a straight, long-barreled gun that would fire far away into our own unknown future.

Ten

Gallup, New Mexico, on the old Route 66 Highway, is a different town than most others in the world—even without an insane mining boom to enhance its notoriety. It is adjacent to the fifteen million acre Navajo reservation surrounded with startlingly beautiful red and cream-colored mesas and bluffs, and is called "The Indian Capital of the World." This landscape has been captured in countless Western films by moviemakers such as John Ford, John Wayne and Hathaway. Movies really left their mark on the town and the world just like uranium would.

In fact, one bartender at the El Rancho Hotel was still telling us about the summer before when film star Robert Mitchum had been harassed by the town bully until he finally asked him outside. Mitchum had dispatched the man with a single left and right combination. If he had won seven Oscars in a row the worship could not have compared to this heroic action. Not in Gallup, New Mexico.

The El Rancho was a grand hotel for the area, having become famous from film stars, notable politicians and assorted entrepreneurs enjoying its spacious frontier type lobby, the fine dining and pleasurable bar and dance floor. Every two or three weekends, Ray and I would rent a couple of rooms there because of all the above and also to simply participate in the gathering of those individuals—both novices and professionals—in this mad arms race that most feared would only end in the destruction of the entire world.

Our rooms here had paintings, curtains, rugs and furniture in pure southwestern colors and decor. We felt right at home as we relaxed through a steak dinner with a Mariachi band roaming about stirring one's drinking blood like a martini shaker.

By eight o'clock when a swing band took over in the bar section, there was a cacophony of uranium related conversations that was growing in intensity and would do so until the two o'clock closing time. Then some of it would continue on in scattered rooms, the lobby and even outside around jeeps and pickups. It was a mixture, from almost every state and country in the world, of dreamers, bottom-feeders and the few experts who I suppose could be found anywhere in gold, diamond or oil booms as well as this radioactive one. There were gringos, from everywhere in the world, Navajo, Zuni and Laguna Indians, Mexicans from south of the border and Spanish-Americans from north of the border, a few blacks and Orientals. It was America. It was America at its worst and at its best right here in this southwestern bar.

No one had a table to himself. Everyone joined in wherever there was an empty chair and visited as if they all had the same name and family. The camp followers (the hookers) are always at boom sites. These ranged from dumpy drunks, to elegantly dressed, enticingly built, experienced ladies of the night—or day for that matter.

Men who work in lonely, mostly silent, places above or below ground hear more than others. I could never keep from overhearing specific conversations in spite of a large blabbing crowd. This gift, or this curse, revealed enormous character studies whether I liked it or not. Without viewing the distracting movements of eyes, mouths, hands and body language, the ability to concentrate on fluctuations of the throat, tongue, and yes, the mind and soul sounds became acute. The intonation of wording told of lies, deceit of close friends, narcissism, greed, fear and self-promotion. In a roomful of tongues, loosened by alcohol and all the previously mentioned traits, a lot of the world was revealed. Immensely varied. Corny. Dumb. Conniving. Brilliant. Naked.

Scatterings from around the room:

> "Son, you'll find only a few people who will actually deliver. Treasure them."
> "I'm tellin' you, Joe, I've found a whole mountain of uranium. High-grade as whipped cream. I'm tellin' you. All I need is a little seed money. Just enough to dig the improvement holes and get a few assays."
> "We seldom see what we have seen."
> "The assays are running from two to ten percent carnotite. Must be a million tons of that in sight. In plain sight! God uh mighty, that'll bring more money than I can count and sure as hell I couldn't live long enough to spend it. That's why I'm gonna let you boys buy in on it. I need help handling the money we're gonna make. I will need lots of help."

At another table . . .

"All women are actresses."
"Yeah, all men think they are."

At a table behind me . . .

"Listen, Sydney, I'm going to sell you twenty
percent of the Jackass Claims for a measly twenty
thousand. I've taken a liking to you. We can work
together. That's why I'm gonna let you in so cheap."

From the stools at the bar . . .

"Quit worrying, Jake, I'm taking out a second
mortgage on my house. That'll be plenty to finish
up the claim work and get started mining."

Ray and I were on our third scotch and we had go-getting
company at our table. One of them was Embree Sonny
Hale, a gold and silver prospector/miner from down south
at Hillsboro, New Mexico. He set his bottle of Pabst Blue
Ribbon beer down on the table and said,

"Hey, Ray, I don't know if you've ever thought about
it before this crazy-ass boom."

Ray waited, but when nothing was forthcoming, he
said, "Thought about what?"

"Optimism." Sonny said, "Overall it causes more pain
than pessimism does." Then he added, "But I kinda break
even. I got both."

A long limbed, droopy-eyed doctorate of social
sciences, who was about two thirds towards reaching his
full drinking capacity, replied to Sonny's remark, "That
is a sorrowful waste of intelligence, sir."

Sonny Hale increased his almost permanent grin by a quarter of an inch, pushed his flat brim hat back over his thick shock of race horse gray hair and without ever blinking, said, "I don't know to whom you are speaking, but I'll take on the responsibility of listening for everyone at this table." Sonny was making quite a sacrifice since there were nine other pairs of ears at this table already.

Alfred, from the university of Pennsylvania, supplied all the words Sonny's ears could handle.

"We esteemed searchers, we seekers of the yellow hued carnotite riches, must form a union of the soul." Alfred downed a double bourbon, licked at his lips and continued. "We are all bound together in a blood bond to save the world from this madness of minds. Tonight I shall make a vow if all here will do the same. I shall relinquish all my mining claims, destroy all property descriptions and assays. It is the only way. We will send emissaries to insist that the Russians do likewise. Any but the most hopeless of fools can see that no one can possibly win this most devilish of competitions."

Sonny being of almost permanent good-nature, agreed—sort of.

"That's right, professor, come on down to Hillsboro and I'll mine gold for you. All I need is plenty of powder and a new jackhammer . . . well, maybe some more mine railing as we go deeper."

Oddly, Sonny's offer was probably one of the few legitimate ones made in the El Rancho Bar that night. He was one of the very rare people in the entire United States who could, with his own hands and eyes, mine gold and make a living at it alone. Even he could see the end coming for individual miners and was becoming damn good at photography.

Alfred had ordered up a round of drinks. He held his glass looking into its brown depths like a fortune teller at a crystal ball. "Gold it is? The same color as carnotite, but which one, my dear fellow, creates the most *e-vil*?" Alfred waited. No response was forthcoming. "Huh? Huh?" He pushed his head forward toward Sonny. "Now there is a question for you to answer."

Sonny said, "My dear, Professor, I do not believe your question is answerable at this time."

A bank teller, built like an Arctic seal, from Madison, Wisconsin, said, "My father advised against the seeking of uranium. He said coal is where the future will certainly be because we will always have cold winters someplace."

Alfred's last double shot had reached the full capacity line, but he had one final statement before he slept sitting up, "If there be a creator of worlds . . . just imagine that maker of eternity concerning himself—or herself—with such trifles as this." And he slept with his hands folded across his chest as if he was about to pray.

Ray reached out and took the hand of a hooker. Getting to his feet, he asked, "Was that last quote from Shakespeare?"

On my fifth scotch and water, I answered, "No. Absolutely not. It must be from Tolstoy. Old Shake had better timing."

I watched Ray bellying up to the blond hooker as they danced to the swing band's rhythm. A little later, I thought, I'll choose one for my own self. There was a girl, about twenty, who had just entered with two others. They were locals. They were not for sale, but I knew if I worked it just right, danced just right, laughed and made them laugh just enough, a freebie was pretty certain.

I ordered a round of drinks for the table and watched

the three sit down. Then I realized why I had noticed the one and not the others. She had that same reddish brown hair of Julie and in a vague way resembled her. I did not look her way again. I did not want the relaxation of the evening ruined so, I tuned my ears to other distractions.

"Hey, Bill, do you think I'm becoming an alcoholic?"

"Naw, you're just a plain old problem drinker."

"Well, shit. I missed another good opportunity then."

"How's that, Rod?"

"Cause I've been drinking ever chance I got for thirty years."

Well now, cheer up. You ain't a failure yet. You got at least another ten years of tryin' left in you."

I was hearing the diverse dialogue again. I could not help myself. It was just there.

"I've been screwin' up my whole life. Now is my chance to make it up to everbody. I got a feeling that this next week is the time I'll make a big strike. Just think about it. I'm going to buy myself a brand new Cadillac, a hundred-dollar suit and I'm gonna drive around and around the town square and ever time I pass the bank, I'm gonna lean out the window and yell, Screw you! Screw you tight ass bastards! Then the next morning I'm going to buy the goddamned bank and fire ever last one of them sons uh bitches. And that ain't all I'm turning down ever loan they apply for just like they did me. Let 'em

eat shit with the chickens like I've had to do."

From the table at my far right . . .

"*You know, Alex, I been meaning to ask you something ever since we left Tulsa to come out here.*"
"*Ask away, Freddie.*"
"*Did I see you actually going to church the Sunday before we left?*"
"*You might have. I sure did go.*"
"*How come? You ain't no church goer.*"
"*Well, Freddie, I spent two days in the blazing sun fixing Reverend Kudrow's roof.*"
"*Well?*"
"*His forty dollar check bounced.*"
"*Everybody mistakenly bounces a check now and then, Alex.*"
"*True, old friend, but six times?*"
"*Surely you didn't dun him for it right there during the services?*
"*No, of course not, I wouldn't do that, but we needed the money real bad to put down on our Geiger counter. So, I endorsed the check again, put it in the collection plate and took out thirty nine dollars.*"

"*How come the odd number?*"
"*I left a dollar for the church.*"
"*Oh.*"

The dance floor was full of couples snuggling and musking up the place. Ray disappeared to his room for about an hour. When he came back I asked him what took so long and he said he forgot to set his clock. I never did figure out what he meant.

There was blabbering and bragging and hoping and crying inside, along with a wild yell of astounding volume every now and then. The musicians were getting a jar full of tips from money mostly borrowed, and a tiny bit actually earned. I loved it all until I had my ninth scotch and stumbled over and asked the Julie-look-alike to dance. She looked me over trying to decide if it was worth it.

I said, "I am a gentleman."

She got up smiling. "I've never danced with one of those before. Let's give it a try."

She did not look nearly as much like Julie as I had thought, but still enough to bother me. She sure knew how to dance, just leaning her breasts, her stomach and her thighs right into every move I made with no strain at all. It was beginning to feel good to both of us, I believe.

I don't know what made me say it, but I did, "Oh, by the way, I'm *not* going to be rich tomorrow."

She tilted her head back thinking about my statement. She said, "Know what? Neither am I."

I said, "It may take me ten years to get rich."

"Why do you think that?"

"Because I work for other people. Arondo Mining."

"Well, at least you work. Most of these poor saps are playing rich when they are broke or getting that way fast."

"Ah, don't blame them too much. Most of them didn't like what they were doing back home anyway. They're just here chasing a few dreams."

"You're just being kind. You really are a gentleman."

"I'm T.C. What's your name?"

"Hi, T.C. I'm Glenna."

"Hi, Glenna."

We moved a little closer together. Just as I was about to make a run at her, three big, old clod-hopping prospectors strode right across the dance floor. They had six-shooters strapped on just like in the western movies they made here in Gallup.

Somebody yelled, "Hey, what you wearing them pistols in here for?"

"Prospecting up on Mt. Taylor. Might run into a bear or a mountain lion."

"There ain't no mountain lions or bears in here."

"You never can tell."

Several people laughed, for some reason.

I felt sorry for the childish poseurs. They thought they were something else, and for a short time—way out here in the lovely, wonderfully-colored uranium country—they were. They truly imagined they were in the old West, playing cowboys and Indians just like they had done as kids. Now they had added a third make-believe—rich miners.

I danced Glenna over closer to the door and holding her soft hand led her outside to our covered jeep. Leaning back against it I pulled her to me and reached under her dress. She tilted her head back and looked me between the eyes. The she decided. She took my hand and slipped it in her panties and I felt her. She pushed in slow circles into my hand, whispering, "Let's get a room and do it right."

I said, "I already have one."

We were halfway down the hall when the soft light from a lamp hit her hair. It glowed exactly like Julie's. Suddenly, just like a bombed bridge, my passion for her collapsed. It was difficult for me to touch her. For God's sake I was denying the very nature of unattached youth.

I stopped and said, "Please forgive me, Glenna. I want you very much. You are truly sweet, but I just can't."

She stood in front of me, her breasts still heaving slightly. "It's okay. Is there someone else? Is that the problem?"

"Yes," I nodded, "But it's not like you think. Please forgive me. Maybe It'll be different later on—another weekend."

To my surprise, she put both her hands lightly on my cheeks and said, looking straight at me again. "It's okay. Really it is. We'll just see what happens."

Jesus, I thought, *after all these months I've let Julie wreck my love, my pride, and even my natural lust. I'm going to have to do something about this blasted horror that has taken away everything.*

More reluctant with each step, I took Glenna back to her table. Her girlfriends were dancing so I sat a minute with her until one of them returned. Then I got up to leave. Since there was nothing I could say, I bowed deeply to Glenna and her companions and walked around looking for Ray and Sonny Hale.

I walked back to the same table just as Sonny returned. All the previous occupants had left and others had taken their places. The constancy of movement here was as sure as the planets.

Sonny was feeling good. We had become close friends.

He was still grinning at least half the time as he said, "You know, T.C., I finally figured out the truth."

As late as the evening had become, I really wanted to hear the truth from an honest man just once.

He continued, "We've got better odds robbing a main street bank than striking gold."

"Or uranium?" I couldn't help adding.

"We're about even there," he said. Then only half-joking, he said, "I ain't had much luck lately prospecting in New Mexico. I'm thinking about trying out Canada."

A wizened, old man of indeterminate, but obviously hard time origin, removed the beer bottle from his lips and said to Sonny in a consoling tone of kindness, "You'll be a lot healthier up north in Canada. The flies are all frozen so stiff they cain't scatter no diseases."

Sonny said politely, "Hey, that's good to know."

"It's a confidence builder," I added for no reason. Then the scattered pieces of the world, gathered here in the El Rancho bar, came uninvited into my ears again.

"Look, old Gunther has got to come down on the 12% royalty before we can sign the papers."

"He'll never do it. That old man knows those claims have at least 800 thousand tons of ore on 'em."

"Listen to me, Hank, you have to show him that the mills will just let him sit there and eat that ore."

"That's just what he'll do. You haven't spent all the time with him I have. My God, I've camped out for days drinking his terrible coffee and eating food that was half lard. I say it again. He'll never give in."

"Everyone ever born has a weak point. He's the most patriotic old fart I ever met. He salutes the toilet before he sits on it. Kinda ease up on him like and tell him how much our country needs this ore for weapons to protect our children. Remind him of all the foxhole suffering he went through in Normandy. Paint a picture of his own children being burned to charcoal by our enemy bombs."

"*Boy, you are a heartless son of a bitch.*"
"*Oh, for shit's sake, Hank, the bomb is not only heartless but souless. Go make the damned deal.*"

From the table behind me . . .

"*I'll meet you at the lawyer's office at nine in the morning. Okay?*"
"*Naw, George, I gotta turn your offer down. It's a generosity I can't afford.*

From somewhere on my left . . .

"*I'm one-third Cherokee on my grandmother's side.*"
"*Listen, it's impossible to be one-third of anything.*"
After a pause, he added, "*You are as white as an albino monkey. You, sir, have swallowed too much whiskey and not enough good, red meat. I'm kinda worried about you.*"
"*Well, please don't say a prayer for me. It might make God real mad.*"
"*I was just thinking . . .*"
"*Please, Henry, don't strain yourself.*"
"*Don't worry. I know my limits. Hey, bartender, set us up another round of doubles over here, and will somebody please slap the grin off that son of a bitch's face. The world just ain't that funny.*"

I was watching a trio sitting at table by the door—two men and a very plain looking woman.

"Emma," he said, *"if you'll tip the band up front, I'll risk a dance with you."*

"Honey," she said, *"I'm not that much of a gambler."*

He punched his buddy and said, "It's amazing how much better looking that girl has got since she's been drinking with us."

From somewhere in the room came a chopped-up mixture of conversations, some were lost by the bar noise that rose and fell like ocean waves and they all ran together . . .

"At least we had the foresight to save up our beans and whiskey for the hard times. I think they might last about as long as we do."

"I'm gonna turn it in. I got a feeling tomorrow's gonna be my lucky day. Yes sir, my really lucky day."

Then the fragmented affliction faded like the end of a broken record with just half sentences essaying into single words. Suddenly there were only sounds with no words. Utterances without understanding. Gone. The reality of voices and faces and all those expressions of the visible human makeup returned.

Sonny was a good-time-catcher. He was out on the dance floor now, delicately doing the two-step with a woman twice his size and enjoying every pound of it.

Ray was back at the table and in a discussion with three geologists from the Atomic Energy Commission. I sat and listened a moment. I had a suspicion about the AEC geologists. A lot of them had flown over massive areas of the western states with their high-powered radioactive detectors called *sinulators* looking for what was called anomalies or hot spots. They would pin down the exact quadrants on their maps and send their professionals in to look where there was at least some uranium. The AEC had already located what would turn out to be two thirds of the major ore bodies before the poor piss-ant prospectors started tearing up the landscape with their pickups, jeeps and walking boots. Of course, in our desperate national effort to surpass the Russians in atomic arms so we could reach that hoped for, prayed for and even craved status of a stalemate, some of the AEC geologists turned information over to private companies— carefully and politically chosen companies.

My little reverie about the AEC boys was broken as I accidentally looked out on the dance floor and saw Julie. My heart damn near froze up solid on me. Then I saw it was Glenna and she was looking at me. I turned my head away, at the same time amazed at my own stupidity.

"Julie, oh, Julie. The thoughts of your deceit and my own self-pitying pain of jealousy hangs in me like an abscessed tooth." It didn't matter how many painkillers I took the agony would return. It had and I was biting down on it. There was only one way it would ever be settled. This obsessive remembering would never leave until it— just like a poisoned tooth—was extracted.

Then my "selective listening ability" suddenly kicked in and saved me for now. When I had explained my strange eavesdropping phenomenon to Julie in a tiny bar in the tiny town of Cerrillos, she had said, 'Maybe you are studying for the wrong profession. Every journalist in the world would love to have that gift.' And I had answered, 'I'm sure a lot of them do.' But she disagreed.

Whatever, however, it was present. I was especially grateful at this moment when I did not want the vision of Julie clouding my mind and I sure as hell did not want to hear the guarded bullshit of the AEC boys.

"Tomorrow, huh?" I heard from two tables away. "I haven't got the time to waste on any more tomorrows. I want it now. I am fast running out of tomorrows."

From another direction came . . .

"I'm getting very disappointed in the human race. I've done everything I can to make it easy for them. I try, I try and I try some more."

"All that trying is admirable, my friend, but delivery is what makes the bread rise."

"We should never worry about the final results of our prospecting. Hellsfire, violence ain't so bad when you're the one dishing it out."

"I've got inside information. You see, fellers,

that's the only kind of information worth having. Inside information, that is. I say let's pool the rest of our money and invest in Hammerstall Energy Corp. The stock's gonna go to three and a half cents by Monday noon and sure as salt in the ocean she'll be a dollar before the month is out."

"Beats doing the digging ourselves. I say let's do it. I'm, too damn old to clamber over one more pile of rocks listening for that damn little Geiger machine to chatter."

"Tomorrow morning it's going to be hard to remember how durn much fun tonight was."

"Fine things are made for fine people."

"Sure, if the fine people have the money to buy them or the skills to steal them."

"My God, you're turning into a cynic and you're not even thirty yet."

The last statement made me think of Julie again so I drank myself deaf.

Eleven

After a very late breakfast of huevos rancheros (blue corn tortillas topped with two fried eggs and smothered with fiery, red chile sauce and a sprinkling of grated cheese) Ray graciously drove us back to Grants. The food had dissipated our dissipation of the night before and it was nice just to sit there and look out at miles and miles of wind and sun sculpted red and cream colored mesas. It didn't even bother me that I knew some of the lighter-hued ones hid the minerals we were paid to chase with such desperate dedication.

As I looked at the awesome beauty surrounding this part of Route 66—"the Mother Road" or "The Road of Flight" as John Steinbeck had so precisely called it—I wondered if those poor downtrodden people in his book had been able to enjoy this awesome beauty even a little bit. Probably not. There was nothing growing there that could fill the hollow places in their bellies. I had a strange deja-vu every time we drove this road. I seemed to recognize the landscape's every crevice and trait, and I saw flashes of people I'd somehow known. I felt like I was living in a parallel world. I was mesmerized.

Americans are the worst, and fastest, people on earth in forgetting their history. They are also the world's most hopeful. Route 66 had certainly changed the course of American history . . . and even some of the rest of the world's. It was not only the main street of America, but it splits New Mexico in half. On the east side of our state, it goes right through Tucumcari, slices through the middle of Albuquerque, does the same on the west side through Grants and Gallup, then on into Arizona and finally ending at the Pacific Ocean after delivering all these desperate souls to California. Thousands upon thousands of families, dispossessed by the great depression and drought, moved hopefully over this fabled route, often a foot or a yard at a time in old cars and trucks that were forever breaking down and blowing tires as they headed West on the Main Street of

America. Movement has always been the real place of American dreams and ambitions. Many died of disease and literal starvation on the way. Others were born on this long road numbered 66. It had been finished in 1926 when everything seemed to be an endless march to paradise in an America prosperous with an unlimited future of dancing and dining. But it was in fact, a remarkable piece of timing. As three of America's most respected prodigies, author John Steinbeck, film director John Ford, and actor Henry Fonda would reveal in "The Grapes Of Wrath" the tragic, sacrificial, dreaming soul of American's heartland on the move.

The so-called Okie migration was America in search of a new beginning-again. The terrible stock market crash, followed by the great depression, then the killing heat and winds of the dust bowl, had sent the desperate men—and especially the women—to the West Coast. There was no way it could be humanly possible, but I felt like I'd made the trip with them.

They arrived at the perfect moment to readily, eagerly, manufacture the goods of war to build our own military forces into the most powerful that had ever walked, rolled and flown over this earth. Our allies—Great Britain, Poland, France and later Russia among others—had already been hammered with terrible ferocity by Hitler's savage forces. The mostly poor, and still disrespected Okies and Arkies were so thankful to have these paying jobs suddenly available to them that they turned out the munitions, tanks, planes and varied necessities of war with enormous and joyful effort. They were unbelievably happy to get paid enough to actually clothe and feed their families, and at the same time, work to help save the world from total dominance and destruction. They did just that. The Okie and Arkie women, followed by others with great rapidity, turned around and changed the position and status of American women from then on. They willingly worked like beavers and expertly produced the munitions of war that created victory for the entire allied effort. Nothing between the sexes and the world would ever be the same.

I thought what an irony it was that because of them and all the warriors of the bloody, brutal battlefields of the world, Ray and I were raised in well-fed comfort.

And now we, too, truly believed that we worked to save the world again, and I was thrilled being a part of all this action worming around us. I loved the earth and the madness of the mining world. Why not? Why not, indeed? At that time in the history of the world, we thought our discoveries would save the planet from annihilation, and that very same ore that made the bombs would create cheap, clean energy so all the world could breathe better in every way. We had been brainwashed to the core. I would soon learn that brainwashing comes in many strange and confusing patterns.

I attempted to conjure up the migrants again and implant them on the new road amidst all this western-movie-beauty. I suddenly felt that their ghosts had to be there, just as I felt the presence of Indians at the white bluff ruins on the San Christobal Ranch.

It all came, fuzzy at first, then there was my Julie and everything materialized. Julie, myself, our three children— two teenage boys and a ten-year-old girl—were pulling the last dead, dry leaves sticking out from endless erratic furrows of sand. The wind was rising and we started walking across what had once been our corn and cotton fields towards a barn that had all the paint sand blasted from it. The wind drove the sand into our eyes, ears, hair, clothes, and lungs. We choked. We coughed. I knew we had to leave this Oklahoma farm one way or another or die. Today would be the last day here.

As Ray drove on parallel to the red mesas, I felt the sand irritate my eyes until I rubbed helplessly at them. The vision was so real, I even tried to dig it out of my ears.

I took a quick glance at Ray. He was in his own world that would remain unknown to me. I easily returned to my Julie. Once I had included her, the imaginations seemed effortless, and blindingly real.

We were feeding the last weeds to two emaciated milk cows, trying to keep them alive till the buyer arrived from town to pay us a few—a very few—dollars for them.

We were on Route 66 now, traveling lighter than most to save gas and tires. The small amount of dollars and pennies in my pocket would have to be stretched like rubber bands. We had left Oklahoma with only our bedding, a kitchen table and chairs, about three changes of clothing—which was all we had anyway—and a few kitchen utensils, which included our big iron cooking pot. Our food supply was a large slab of sowbelly bacon, a half sack of pinto beans, and a box of hard, dry biscuits that Julie had spent most of the day cooking. Two canvas bags held our water and that was about it, except for my old twenty-two rifle that had kept us going until there wasn't a rabbit, squirrel, or wild prairie creature left in our entire county.

Julie looked at the battered gas station map and said, "We're about forty miles from Flagstaff, Arizona, now. We'll rest there for the day."

I knew she was thinking about the great stretch of desert we would start dropping down to soon after Flagstaff. I reached over and took her warm hand. She looked up from the map and smiled at me through hidden tears. Even so, that smile and those blue eyes made me melt a little inside and steel my resolve to deliver our family safely across the killing desert to the great oasis—California.

And now our little family was less than a hundred miles from conquering the desert when a tire blew out and the old Ford's radiator ran out of water. I pulled to the side of the road into the bar ditch, jumped out, jerked my shirt off wadding it up to unscrew the radiator cap hoping it would prevent serious scalding of my hand.

Here we were. No spare tire—we had used up our last one in Winslow. It was two days of waving other weary travelers down, trying to beg a spare and some water. They couldn't help. They were in the same condition as us. We did get enough water to keep us alive, but no tire. I had enough money to possibly buy one, but then that would leave us flat-broke and helpless, at the mercy of others when we arrived. We could hold out as long as we had a tiny bit of food and a few drops of water left, but they were soon gone.

On the second day, I stopped a couple in their thirties. They pulled their Ford truck to a stop beside us. My eyes went to the two large canvas bags of water hanging on the truck stakes, and the two extra tires that were in plain sight. No matter what, I didn't intend to let them leave us stranded any longer. I also couldn't bring myself to hand them our last few dollars.

The couple said, with what I believe was sincere regret, that they must be going. My body seemed to sink into my chest in a hot bar-ditch causing my breath to come with great strain. All seemed lost, then my Julie came forward with my rifle and box of shells. I thought, "My god, she's going to rob them, but instead she offered it to them in a trade for enough water for the radiator and ourselves, a tire, and a box of crackers. The precious rifle that had so many times saved our lives had just done it again for the last time. It was mixed happiness, but would allow us to arrive at the oasis with some money in our pockets.

Then, like a montage in a movie, it all speeded up.

We worked in a winery. I became a field supervisor. Our children all earned scholarships to college, and Julie taught part-time at a Napa Valley school. We prospered, but above all we loved.

Then, in our mid-years we had our own grape arbors with a large comfortable home where we contracted all our grapes for years ahead to the famous winery I had labored at so successfully. Often in the still evenings, my Julie and I would sit out on a our porch and gaze across the golden light of late day at the purple hills we called mountains and talk of our children, and then our new grandchildren, while we sipped the finest wines from our patron.

Julie and I traveled the world for a year, and felt right at home in Old Prussia and Paris, but when we took a tour down the Nile River of Egypt we felt most at home of all. We made many vows to return to that place that felt as familiar as our great back porch looking across the valley of Napa. We never did return, but we didn't need to. We were happy here now, watching a hawk circling above the vineyards as he looked down on the world and us. Julie's eyes smiled with that haunting look of knowledge, of unspoken things and place, without measured time.

Then I was sitting beside my partner, Ray, looking down the highway as we pulled into the edge of Grants and back to the *now* world. Was it a day-dream? Was it a vision? Was it a revelation? Maybe part of all three. I clasped my hands together and felt it. I rubbed at my cheek and felt it. I craved to talk about it to Julie. I even wished I could verbalize it all to Ray. I could do neither. A lonely pain soaked into my chest. Sometime soon though, at the deadliest moment of my life, my mind would be more open and the many truths and verifications would be revealed. The real truth is always the action leading up to the facts.

Ray suddenly said with real concern in his voice, "You know, T.C., that some of those AEC guys are peddling classified anomalies?"

"No. How do you know that?" I asked.

"They're driving really expensive cars and spending money with total abandon."

"Aw, hell, Ray. You and I are doing the same thing. Okay, so you are driving us home in an Arondo Mining pickup and we don't own real expensive cars. We're still spending money like irrigation water."

"Yeah, I know, but there's a difference. I can just tell. There's a difference. We know when we've overstepped. We know when we're broke. Those guys have no concern about the things that we ordinary folks do. It's different. I can tell." Ray said.

"Right now I don't give a damn about any of that stuff. I just want to get back out on the mesas in the morning and start working," I said. "By the way, did we make it to the genius hour?"

"Genius hour?"

"Yeah. Haven't you ever noticed that every drinker in the world turns into a genius at three o'clock in the morning?"

"Oh yeah," he said, shaking his head carefully in agreement, "we made it all right but I gotta tell you, that extra thirty minutes we put in calls for a cup of hot, black coffee, right now."

He pulled the truck into a parking place in front of the Drillers' Cafe. We found a booth and the waitress had two cups of scalding coffee in front of us before we had time to think about our hangovers and she did it with a smile.

"Now what else can I get you?" she asked.

Ray said, "That's all for now." Then before she got halfway to the next table, he said, "I think I better have a glazed doughnut. I feel the need for about a bucket of sugar."

I nodded and pointed at myself, "Me, too."

Then I asked Ray, "Who does she remind you of? She reminds me of somebody, but I can't come up with it."

Ray shook his head, "Beats me. Nobody I can think of."

Then it gradually came back—she looked like the nurse who took care of me at St. Joseph's Hospital while I recovered from the head injury Ray helped me get. I couldn't remember her name, but I'd never forget the tenderness and caring she gave me. I decided quite awhile back that the world would be a pretty sorry place—indeed impossible to live in—if it weren't for good nurses and good waitresses. They were always giving people relief in some form or another. And what thanks did they get for it? Callus, tendentious and aching bodies and damn poor tips, generally.

"Lois!" I blurted out.

"Lois? Lois who?"

"The nurse who the waitress reminds me of." Ray shrugged and I said, "Oh, never mind." I went back to silently praising nurses and waitresses and marveling at what our civilization would be like without them. We'd be thirsty and hungry, neglected when we're sick. The business world would come to a virtual standstill if we had to stop and make sandwiches for everybody we were talking deals with. And think about all the hospitals on the globe. There were civilian hospitals, hospitals in the desert, in the jungle, in war, oh, my God, the list is endless. We'd never make it. I wished I could share all this enthusiastic knowledge with Ray, but I knew it would be totally wasted on him today. Anyway, the thoughts had helped my hangover and I would definitely plunk down a sizeable tip when we left.

I looked over at Ray and started doing some dreaming in certain reality. I said, "I wonder if we should do a little thinking about headquartering in Denver when we finally get our firm established?" Then added, "Of course, I'd hate to leave Albuquerque, but Denver would be more in the center of mining in the west. What do you think?"

"Yeah, it would be a little better for expansion in the western half of the U.S. but we've always . . . well, since we were in junior high, anyway . . . talked about going international. I don't see any reason to lower our aim now," he said.

"You're right. If we're operating worldwide it won't make any difference where our headquarters are located. We can have branch offices anywhere."

"You know, T.C., I can't help thinking about what professor Gill told us." I waited, he continued, "Don't you remember? He said that only one tenth of one percent of the world's gold is all that had been mined. Hell, that's got to apply to all other minerals as well."

"Stands to reason. Old professor Gill had a way about him . . . a way of making you ponder beyond the books. I forget now what it was, but he had me thinking that the most massive deposits of copper and other minerals would be found far south in places like Peru, Brazil or Guatemala."

"Aw, shit, T.C., you're not fooling me. You just want to get down there and explore some of those Mayan and Aztec ruins."

"Hey, you been reading the telegrams of my mind again? What I said was, 'there is an abundance of wealth there that's already been mined and turned into precious works of art.'"

Ray said, only half joking, "Everybody at school and Arondo Mining thinks you are going to make a geologist of international reputation. And I know it, too, but I somehow can't help wondering if I won't catch you taking night classes in archeology some time before long."

"Not to worry, ol' amigo. I'll not be doing anything different until we are established in at least half the world."

The waitress kept our cups full without interrupting while we were having all this bullet dodging palaver and as we got up to leave we both left a sizable tip.

It had been difficult for me to sit with Ray in this world that my Julie inhabited without being able to feel her touch, and in return touch her as I felt and dreamed I had in the other worlds of Paris, the great Nile River, and on our own front porch in Napa Valley.

Twelve

I think it was about three weeks later when Ray said, "How about going home for the weekend, T.C.? I think I'm falling in love with . . ."

His falling permanently in love was about as likely as

the Resurrection coming during the next World Series.

"I can't," I lied, "I have a date with Glenna."

I don't exactly know why I lied, but a day or so later I sort of figured it out. I just did not want to be back in Albuquerque with Ray and risk running into Julie. I hadn't had the courage to tell my folks what had really happened between us, so they still thought it was truly possible we'd get back together. Julie had visited me in the hospital and shown much tenderness, but when I was better she never came again—that I know of. Maybe I lied because I thought it would cause a rift in the long-term friendship my folks had with Julie's parents. The truth would create a domino effect among our friends. Once a deep friendship like mine and Ray's was altered and known about, its detrimental effect would ripple out in wide circles.

Ray asked, "Glenna? Who is Glenna?"

"You know. She's the girl I was dancing with at El Rancho the other night."

He strained back and then said, "Oh yeah, I remember now. She kinda reminded me a little bit of . . ." and he got all nervous, "of my cousin . . . my cousin Alicia in Santa Fe. You remember Alicia?"

I knew he almost said Julie and I also knew he did not have a cousin in Santa Fe by any name whosoever. "Naw, don't remember her."

After Ray left town, I tried to rectify my lie about Glenna. I called information for Glenna Shorheim. To my surprise, I got it.

She answered, "Glenna here."

"Hey. Hi. This is T.C. You probably don't remember me, but we danced and visited awhile at El Rancho awhile back."

There was a silence.

"Glenna? Are you there?"

"Yes. Yes, I remember you, T.C., but I never thought I'd hear from you again."

"Well, I feel a little silly about my problem the other night. I was hoping you'd forgive me and I could take you to see *The African Queen*. You know, with Katherine Hepburn and Bogart? Have you seen it yet?"

"Actually, I haven't. I don't remember now, but I somehow missed it."

"Me, too. They're having an encore showing at the Sunshine in Albuquerque this weekend. Would you like to go?"

There was a hesitation and then she said with much sincerity, "I'd really love to."

I was suddenly relieved. I anxiously told her I would drive to Gallup from Grants and pick her up and we would go to the second matinee and have dinner afterwards. She seemed pleased, too.

She made things better by offering, "I'll just meet you in Grants to make it easier. There is no need for you to drive all the way over here and then back. A waste of time and that's all we have."

"I'll meet you at the coffee shop on Highway 66," I agreed, then we can leave your car at my apartment."

"Sounds good."

It all came off without a hitch. We drove across the vast, broken land of central New Mexico. With each mile closer to the city, the great dragon-backed spine of the Sandia Mountains got bigger and less blue as the massive rock spires revealed their natural gray-brown colors.

We had made a little small talk, which I'm about as

skilled at as a poodle pulling a wagon-load of bricks.

"Well, you know I'm a mining engineer and I work for Arondo Mining. Did I tell you that the other night?"

"No."

"Do you have a job? If it's not too rude for me to ask."

"Of course not. I'm a bookkeeper for Anaconda Mining in their branch office in Gallup."

"I knew we had things in common—but my gosh, we both work for mining companies."

She pushed back her auburn hair on one side and said with a suddenly on and suddenly off brazen and very quick smile, "I hope we have more in common than that."

"I'm sure we do."

I did have another form of ease with her though. There was a warm sensuality to her that could not be denied. I felt it, and I knew she did, too. I looked forward to our night out with a comfortable desire. There are worse things than comfort. There are also better things than comfort. Right now, comfort would do.

We got parked and I held her warm, soft hand as we walked to the ticket office at the Sunshine. We both wanted buttered popcorn and a coke. Things were matching up better now.

The theater was only about a quarter full for this second showing on Saturday afternoon. The kid with the flashlight directed us to seats about halfway down. A newsreel was on. A volcano was erupting and killing a bunch of people somewhere in Italy. By the time the shifting and arranging popcorn, cokes and buttocks was done, the movie was on.

I thought about a third through the movie, that I was enjoying this date much as I had during my recent boyhood. I was in this very same theater, doing the same popcorn eating, washing the little hulls down with coke to keep from choking, enjoying the picture immensely and thinking about kissing the girl by my side. As always. Would it never change?

When Bogie and Hepburn see the torrents of churning water driving the leaky old boat toward the waterfall and certain doom, Glenna grabbed my hand and clamped down with the amazing strength of adrenaline-charged blood. When they had safely maneuvered the deadly current, her hand relaxed in mine. I squeezed hers and she signaled me back with a soft pressure. I repeat: Would it never change?

Yes. Without understanding the spiritual laws, the laws of mathematics, or the laws of impossible odds, my eyes were suddenly three seats forward on the heads of two women. My guts turned to both chilled and sour mash. My hand was almost instantly sweating into Glenna's. It couldn't be, but it was. There sat Julie and her mother. Could it be that she too, had missed the showing of *The African Queen* when I had broken our date to study for my finals . . . and . . . and had entrusted my best friend to escort her to the show? Of course, Ray had taken her out drinking, instead, and she had spread her lovely long legs for him in the back seat of his car. Damn, I should have read those letters.

Suddenly, I wanted to scream out curses at fate, at Ray, at Julie, at God. I glanced sideways at Glenna. She caught it and with a very kind and pleasing smile squeezed my hand again.

God! God! God! I prayed to myself with a mighty struggle to keep it in. You've put me in this unforgivable position so at least give me the strength to control the multiple emotions vibrating through my brain and body.

The movie was over, but the theater was still dark. Julie and her mother moved in silhouette against the screen toward the aisle. Even here, in one of the most awkward movements in the world—getting past seats and knees to the aisle of a movie house—Julie's motion was fluid, hypnotic, elegant. Oh God, again.

No matter what hatred I had for her deceit, the soul around my heart warmed and melted in a strange and terrible ache. She was right here in the flesh that should have been my flesh. Somehow I fought away the singular numbness.

Hiding, I bent over to pick up the coke cups and popcorn bags. Moving my hands around searching desperately for other litter until the overwhelming presence of Julie had passed. Oh God, it wasn't over. I actually could smell her entrancing musk as she walked up the aisle. The place had people with perfume, people with body odor, hair shampoo, hand lotion, the scent of newly polished shoes, the smell of popcorn to name a few, yet past them all I smelled my Julie alone as a bloodhound does the scent of an escaping prisoner in a forest with a million other obvious odors.

I sat back up feeling like I was dissolving into the cushioned seat. I couldn't move for a few moments. Glenna was getting her purse ready and had also neatly placed her coke container inside the popcorn bag. She was ready to go, but she waited. I still didn't move, so she waited some more with unmoving patience. She was a fine woman. I couldn't dismay or hurt her again just because my lost love had by the most remotest of chance been present. It was none of Glenna's doing, and she must not be made to pay for my own debt. No. I had to stall for time so Julie and her mother would be out of the theater and out of the parking lot. I leaned around and gently took her face in one hand and kissed her soft, soft lips. She helped. She tasted like raspberry sherbet and it was her scent I so urgently inhaled now. The soothing scent of offering.

I was lost in a fog of delicious horror. I leaped up and without explaining to Glenna, much less myself, rushed to the aisle and started making my way through and around the bodies heading for the exit. It was a rudeness of desperation that caused me to jostle and actually move people aside by hand. I had to get out and confront Julie. I had to apologize now for being so callously unforgiving. I had to hold her to me so close she could feel my heart telling her the truth of my love for her. I had to look into those haunting eyes that seemed to have lived forever and knew all the secrets of the galaxy's past and present. I had to see deep into the windows that smiled their turquoise bemusement at both the inner and outer dimensions.

When I at last made the lobby, I breathed for the first time since I had left my seat. The scent of popcorn went unnoticed. I rushed to the street weaving through the couples of all ages who were standing and visiting about the film, moving erratically towards their transports in the parking lot. How could they all be so casual when my very essence was at stake?

Then I saw them. Julie's mother was at the wheel. I raised an arm and my throat prepared to yell and stop them before they made it to the street. At this instant a delivery van from a flower shop pulled in front of me. I almost ran into it face first. I dodged around the rear of the van only to run into another car that had pulled up beside it. I cleared that and raced after Julie's car just as it was pulling away.

I yelled as loudly as my body would allow, "Julie!" and then again. It was too late. I got a glance, as another car's headlights flashed through theirs, of Julie tossing her thick, auburn hair and turning toward her mother, talking. I knew she was speaking fondly of the movie. Tears came into my eyes as suddenly as shock. It should have been me she was telling her favorite scenes to.

I stood there until I realized that a car was honking angrily at me to get the hell out of the way. I felt a terrible loss and didn't care if they wanted to run over me.

Finally, I took a couple of very deep breaths and made my way back into the theater and down the aisle explaining in some way to the usher that I had forgotten something. I had. My date.

Glenna sat staring unmoving at the screen, waiting. I took her hand and said, "I'm embarrassed." Since my actions were impossible to explain, I continued, "I had a rush call to the restroom."

"Please don't worry about it," she said. "It gave me time to think about the film."

I was very thankful for her kindness after my rudeness. She made things easier and I had to do my best not to forget it. I felt better already.

We drove back west down Central Avenue and 66 to the Sunset Inn for dinner. The place was beginning to fill up. This was a politicians' hangout. The steaks were as good as they were anywhere and the enchiladas were famous—so was the swing orchestra.

We had two margaritas with our dinner, and although I cannot remember exactly what we talked about it went smoothly, and so did the dancing in the soft lighting of the adobe restaurant. Thanks to the hot food and warm music, everyone was beginning to laugh and talk freer, and dream and flirt and con. It was an evening blessed, or stolen, in time.

We stayed until the two o'clock closing and when we got to my apartment in Grants, Glenna undressed without a word and stretched out on the bed raising her arms out to me saying simply, "Come." I did.

I woke up the next morning late realizing Glenna was gone. I found a note on a torn grocery sack. It said:

"My dear, T.C.,
Thank you for one of the best evenings of my life. I don't know how I know, but I do, that you are still attached to someone. You removed it with great struggle and gave sixteen hours of your life to me. Thank you. Maybe someday we will meet again, but not now. You do understand, I know.
Love just the same,
Glenna"

I knew I had lost another love before it had moved past the garden gate. Does nothing ever change?

Thirteen

At first, Ray and I worked with experienced geologists mapping out the drilling holes. Then we were slowly shifted into actual hands-on work on our own. As we, and the Indians, labored to help deliver the power that could blow up the world, the uranium prospectors quit the hills, the bars and the restaurants and returned to whatever was normal in their widely scattered hometowns—mostly slow times. They put their lives, their families and their dissipated fortunes back together. Even though they seldom talked about it because of their foolish losses, it was the very highest time of their lives.

Ray and I had a growing pride in being involved in the "delivery part" of the prospectors' boom. The boom, boom, blooey part did not affect us too much. Our careers were moving onto pretty solid ground. I felt considerable satisfaction with the way my life was going. Well, fairly satisfied. I still thought about Julie more than I wanted to. In fact, I couldn't admit it yet, but there was a hole in my heart that seemed unfixable.

Our contracted work was ahead of schedule. Those of us who were the explorers had really begun to believe we were helping save our wondrous world. We felt good about what we were doing to the point of elation.

Every other week Ray and I got Wednesday and Thursday off. We shared a rented apartment in Albuquerque so we could visit our parents and old friends without imposing on any of them. I tried, and mostly succeeded, to avoid Julie. Whenever I would see her driving somewhere or going into a store, or walking along a sidewalk, I would duck my head and turn away, when in buried truth I wanted to race after her with all the speed I could gather.

I know none of this sounds reasonable.

I could face other challenges, big challenges, huge problems, but I could not deal with this Julie situation with any logic or reasoning even though I had long ago convinced myself that I was a rational man. I also blinded myself into believing that I had completely forgiven Ray for his little fling with my woman. As I would gradually find out, the person easiest to lie to is yourself. Fools average out in the world of odds more plentiful than geniuses.

I had been in the First National Bank of Albuquerque downtown to make a deposit and exited on to Central Avenue when I saw Julie head on. She had just stepped out of her father's construction company office across the street. We both stood as if paralyzed upright and stared at each other. Her face seemed to jump across the traffic at me. Her wide turquoise eyes spoke silently, hauntingly. There was a tortured question in them. Something that stirred my confused soul like a cake mixer.

Suddenly I wanted to leap across the traffic and pull her so close that our clothing would vanish. It was an anguished sweet pain that I would never forget. It was probably only a moment that we stood transfixed, but her eyes had spoken of loss. Great loss.

There had been a question in her expression that I did not understand—a question that would strain me mightily to comprehend. But when the answer finally came, I did know. And when it did, I wished it hadn't.

We turned away. I did not look back as I sought the safety of my parked car. I sat there behind the wheel staring down the crowded street wanting to cry. When tears are shed inwardly they turn to acid. Acid is always hungry.

Back on the sandstone mesa of Grants, the memory of Julie would begin to recede slowly, very slowly indeed.

Fourteen

Ray had a date with Alice again, and he suggested that if I'd like to call Glenna we could all have dinner and drinks at the Sunset Inn in Albuquerque. He spoke of Alice with such surprising respect that curiosity caused me to relent.

"Sure, if you'll take me by myself," I said, "'Cause Glenna is out of town this weekend."

"Of course, we'd love to have you. I know Alice would like to see you again."

Since it seemed as if I was supposed to know Alice, I started to ask who she was. Then I figured I could control my suspense. I dropped it.

We drove to Alice's apartment in Corrales. Ray usually just honked and waited for his dates, but this time he got out and knocked on the door. It opened for a moment, they spoke briefly, then he waited on the little adobe porch until she came out.

With one hand he eased her out in front of him as they came toward the car. My God! Alice, as it turned out, was the nurse from St. Joseph's whose face and name were forever branded into my brain as . . . Lois? Ray surely knew this when I was searching for her name the other day in the coffee shop, but he had said nothing.

I jumped out of the car to meet her as Ray was saying "T.C. Young, you remember Alice Farney, don't you?"

"Yes. Yes. How are you, Alice? It's great to see you. How have you been?"

That pretty well took care of my chitter-chatter. No matter, Ray was a master at it and Alice's profession demanded that skill.

"It is wonderful to see you again, T.C. You're looking fit."

"Hey, I feel great." I somehow choked out.

"Well, you should," Ray said, "Alice saved your cockeyed life, old friend."

Alice gave a slight roll to her eyes and said, "He keeps giving me all the credit. But it was you yourself, T.C., and a good doctor, and the luck of having so many people who love you."

"Don't listen to that modesty, T.C. She managed the entire recovery." Ray said firmly.

Somehow beyond my recall we got off the subject of me, and the next thing that mattered was the comfort of a Sunset Inn Margarita and some real New Mexico red. Their steaks were great here, too—everybody said so—and each time I came I intended to have one, but no matter what, that subtle odor of chile instantly altered my craving and the red chile enchiladas with a fried egg in the middle, topped with shredded lettuce and bits of fresh tomato, won me over.
Ray had started out the evening opening doors and pulling out chairs for Alice with eagerness and care for her every need. I had never seen him give anyone such attention. She was just as pleased with all of it as I was dumbfounded.

They both seemed to enjoy carrying on a conversation without saying very much that I could understand, or needed to for that matter. But, of course, that's the way it is between lovers—and I assumed they were—because they used a language that only they understood fully. I was thankful that they were both experts in that field.

I was starting my second Margarita and the swing music was becoming more velvety by the minute. I watched Ray and Alice glide on the dance floor as if they were sewed together. A rare bliss.

I got up and asked a lovely Spanish lady from a table of girls to dance. She was good at this swing and I figured she must be older than she looked to have such finesse at this soon-to-be old time music—derisively called slow dancing by the young. I had forgotten for a moment that I was still young, myself. Real lost love does that to you.

I was relaxing just the same. I returned Carmen to her table, thanked her and asked if we could try another later. She smilingly agreed, and I felt ready for one of those special evenings.

Ray brought Alice back to our table, seated her and excused himself to the boys' room. Alice fondly watched him disappear, then turned to me glowing.

"T.C., I did my best with your concussion, but in spite of what Ray says I felt I wasn't getting anywhere at all. I could tell the doctors felt the same way." After a quick glance in the direction of the men's room, she continued. "Well . . . I . . . it was your Julie who really turned you around. Every time she'd visit, you would have longer and longer lucid spells."

The emotions in my pounding skull and my stomach were suddenly in such turmoil that I was certain I would simply expire.

Then, as if from a barrel across the room, I heard Alice say, "I think she loves you very much and I know you would have recovered even sooner if Julie hadn't become ill and couldn't continue her visits."

"Ill?" I somehow managed to utter.

"Ray said she was ill—that her liver problems were serious. He said they were taking her to a friend who is a specialist in Santa Fe. It always pays to have a doctor for a friend." She gave a slight chuckle. "I hope she is fully recovered," she added.

Ray returned.

I died, right there in the Sunset Inn, many agonizing deaths in the next few moments. I couldn't figure what in hell to say. The relaxing time had switched to a deadly time. A certain statement or an extra word of a certain kind could lead to instant violence.

Then I realized the conversation had gone on to Colorado where both their families had mountain cabins. I didn't dance anymore. I did drink many more margaritas, and the counting thereof was not important enough to indulge in.

I don't recall how we decided to leave, but I do remember how surprised and in some unexplainable manner, pleased I was when Ray walked Alice to her front door and gave her a light kiss and a big hug. He returned to the car and settled in behind the steering wheel. "We're saving it all until we're ready to get married. No matter how long it takes," he explained, unnecessarily.

I could hardly believe that I said, "Good. Good boy." But I did. This evening had revealed that my life long friend was a far more complex son of a bitch than I had realized. I wasn't sure yet what I would do about all this, but I knew I would do something. I had no choice.

A couple of days later I called my mom when I knew dad would be at work. After a few minutes I casually asked her about Julie's health. Mom (who had said so often to dad, "Those kids are made for one another" that I thought about trying to copyright the statement) was puzzled, but very pleased at my interest in Julie's well being. She called back and said that Julie was wonderfully healthy. In fact, she had not had so much as a cold in three years. All I could do was thank her. I know she was puzzled at the deep confusion I tried to hide in my voice, when she had just given me such good news.

Fifteen

The work was winding down at Arondo as far as uranium exploration was concerned. We had lucked out in our lives and careers by graduating straight into fine paying jobs of great import. Everyone was feeling the joy of succeeding at their first major work of world consequence. Even the older geologists were as excited as we beginners. A banner time it was.

We all had a big laugh when we heard of the Utah miner who had dug a six-hundred-foot tunnel into uranium slightly too-low-grade for milling. He had a scheme to charge people a dollar a head to come into his tunnel and sit for an hour. They did it because somehow the word had spread that an hour spent there would free them of arthritis for three years. The middle aged and the elderly were standing, sitting, or lying in line for half a mile to buy their dollar-day bargain. The old miner and his family got financially well before some doctor ruined their fun by publicly announcing that radiation was harmful to your health. But no harm done; not one of the clients could have possibly lived long enough to be hurt by the small amount of radiation.

They had started drilling right behind our mapped out programs. Fortunately the core drills revealed a very minable grade of ore. It may have been pure luck but we got credit for good luck as if it were brilliance.

Yes, what a time it was!

The work Ray and I turned in had been rated excellent and we were offered a renewal on our contracts to continue our work up in Utah, but we politely refused, having made other plans. We accepted, instead, a one-year contract to map out an additional open-pit ore area around the huge Molybdenum Corporation of America mine north of Taos between Red River and Questa, just south of the Colorado border.

We rented a room in the Taos Inn and gladly made the eighty-mile round trip each day. When we first rented it, I was reluctant because of the treasured memory of sharing this special place with Julie. Ray liked it. It was convenient and comfortable. I simply had to deal with those old feelings. What's the old saying? "Get back on the horse that throwed you."

It was high-country work on the mostly treeless mining area surrounded by heavy forest and a high portion of the Rocky Mountain range. We had to climb across large areas of decomposed granite where there were billions of little pebbles that made it extremely difficult to keep one's footing. It was like trying to walk across a room full of marbles. One wrong slip here would send us sliding towards a precipice of no return.

We did have several falls, but we somehow grabbed a twig, a crevice or something to hold on to. The palms of our hands and our knees were sore and scabbed all the time from the scraping and bruising we took from these countless tumbles.

Then it happened. In spite of all our caution, I literally felt Ray fall about thirty or forty yards above me. I turned my eyes uphill just as he started sliding.

"Flatten out!" I screamed into the freezing wind, "Spread your legs and your arms!"

He did, but the momentum was already too great and he started gaining instant speed. In a glance I estimated that I was standing about twenty yards from the edge of a sheer drop off of hundreds of feet. There is no way anyone has figured out how the human brain can, under great pressure, move the body's reasoning power and its muscles with such speed that it would embarrass a comet, while at the same instant actually make the world turn into slow motion. It only seems to happen when a fraction of a second is the difference between living or dying.

I judged where Ray would pass me, and I moved to intercept, at the same time I saw a scrub bush perhaps a foot high. I leapt sideways, grabbed the bush with one hand, and braced—like the left guard I used to be in football—to ease the impact of another body by charging at it first with my own.

Ray's body was twisted to the side at about a two-thirds angle when we hit. It became a blur, of course, as we collided. I was addled but somehow slowed him, getting hold of his belt and his pants straining far beyond my actual strength to grab the bush with the other hand. It worked for an immeasurable instant. Then the bush tore loose and we both started gathering speed in a slide to the great unknown.

I saw the deep indentation and swung both of us half around, sticking my legs with the toes up straight out in front. It was a hell of a sudden stop. It felt like my legs had driven my ass up on my shoulders. Ray's body kept on moving to the length of my arm. I was sure it was now at least a foot longer than the left one. But, by damn, we were stopped about a dozen feet from the space where only birds fly.

I was pretty confused after that, but I crawled and Ray crawled with me. I held his belt until we were out of the granite marbles. Then somehow I found the trail and got him down to the Jeep and loaded in.

I drove right on past the great mill and the mine super's office and floor-boarded the Jeep all the way to Taos and the Holy Cross Hospital where a doctor took care of Ray.

It was getting dark, so I asked a nurse when I could see Ray. She said they would be through with the X-rays and other tests in about an hour. I decided to go to the hotel and get calmed down.

I sat down and stared at a Santo in a niche. Suddenly I smelled the sweet warmth of the Napa Valley I'd envisioned that day Ray drove me back to Grants from the El Rancho party in Gallup. I saw the white marble nude sculpture by a very famous Paris artist. I recalled that I'd paid a fortune for it—two years of winery grapes—and felt it worth ten times that. It had cost me more than our entire European tour. The eyes turned turquoise as Julie's did in a certain light. Suddenly, the beckoning hand of the sculpture reached out to me and closed around my soul. I saw the marble nude seem to become Julie's precious flesh and then I was back to the Santo of St. Jude in the adobe niche again. I felt healed a bit . . . ready for any challenge.

When I returned to Holy Cross, Dr. Pond was gone, the nurse was smiling so I knew before I saw him that ol' Ray Morris would live on for awhile at least. He was all painted with iodine and bandaged from his shins to his upper thighs, and his arms and hands as well. His face was swelled quite a bit and there were some bad scrapes, but no stitches.

He said drowsily through the fog of whatever medicine they were draining into him, "Hey, partner, you saved my worthless life."

"You're really okay?"

"I think so. They won't tell me anything for sure."

I said, "I have a feeling you'll live long enough to grow up after all."

He got serious. "Don't make jokes about it. I owe you my life, dammit."

"Okay. You can pay me later."

Before I could pull up a chair, he was asleep. The nurse told me that they wanted to keep him two or three days to observe if there was any internal bleeding. If not, he could be released.

I said, "Do you mean to tell me, nurse, that he doesn't have anything broken? Not even one little bone?"

"Miraculously."

"Well then, please give me a sledge hammer." She looked puzzled. I continued, "I just gotta break at least one of his bones. It is simple justice."

She looked startled, then realized I was joking and giggled weakly. I guess working with the real thing all the time, she failed to find any humor in my suggestion. Instead, she started trying to check out all *my* scrapes and bruises. I protested, but she sat me down, cleaned my hurts and put some medicine on them that burned like hell. My own injuries were minor, but I sure was sore the next day.

Ray was in a solid sleep now, so I drove back to the plaza, had chile rellenos for lunch at La Cocina, then moseyed slowly up toward the Kit Carson House Museum. Since I love paintings and other art work, I decided, if I moved with enough caution, I could make it up to Gallery A and take a look at someone else's painted views of the high country Ray and I lived, worked and almost died in.

I abstractly saw this white Cadillac parked in front of the gallery. Three figures got out and moved toward the entrance. Then I focused in with a jarring intensity. It was Julie and her parents. Her father was holding the door open for the two women. He was taking them into the gallery where Julie and I had become so completely entranced with the eclectic southwestern paintings—the very place where we had secretly purchased each other a work of art.

I wanted to escape. I wanted to become invisible. I wanted to jump up on the roof of the adobe office building next door and hide. I wanted to duck my head, whirl and run, but I could not move. Everything that worked on me had locked up. What kind of coward was I? Would nothing ever change?

Julie said something to her father. He took a quick, embarrassed glance at me before stepping inside ahead of his daughter.

Julie stood squared away towards me. She ever so slowly walked forward. Then the terrible hurt inside made the granite bruises, cuts and scrapes feel like the pinch from a newborn baby. The ignorant, blinding pain of jealousy defeated me. I turned away the moment I looked into those liquid blue-green eyes where I had so often felt I could swim.

I didn't feel my legs moving but I knew they were because the perpetual image of Julie was getting closer, bigger, more beautiful. Then we were so close I could feel the vibrations of her being and smell her unique essence. Then her eyes swallowed me. I saw her damp lips moving and thought I heard sounds, but it was my own voice uttering the most common of all great truths.

"Julie. Goddamn it, I love you more than ever."

"I know," she answered in a whisper, "Oh, God, do I know."

Our hands slowly moved out and touched. The electricity of physical contact propelled our bodies together and we were kissing in starvation. Then jealousy, vanity, or madness jerked me away from her and all I could see were her naked legs on each side of Ray's broad back— and I was blinded.

I whirled, running, almost falling between two buildings into an alley and headed back to the safety of La Cocina. I had two scotches and water—one fast, one slowly. After the shock of seeing her subsided, I craved to go back and find her.

I drove all over Taos looking for the white Cadillac, but she was lost to me. Julie was gone. I felt cowardly and dumber than cracked cement as I returned to my room to hide from the world.

In a week or so, Ray and I were back on the mountain. Slowly, we conquered our fears and went on with our work. It took us a month longer than it should have to map this section.

It was an open winter and in spite of the frigidity of the ceaseless winds we were able to work around the light, shifting snow. The drilling program that followed our mapping brought up core drills with good quality ore over a wide area. I suppose any other geologist or mining engineer could have done as well, but that did not matter, it was *our work* and would be forever known as such.

There were years of work and wages ahead now for the Hispanic miners who lived at nearby Questa. They were the best possible. After all they had had almost four hundred years of ancestral experience at the mining game—The longest in America. Molybdenum was critical in the hardening of metals that made up the U.S. manufacturing base and, the gray, slick, greasy-feeling ore helped make rockets and cannon barrels as well as automobiles and refrigerators. Even so, the national economy controlled the welfare of the people of this mine and consequently the immediate area.

Sixteen

Ray and I finished our program at MolyCorp (as the miners had named it) and our big chance came, but Ray wanted to take a few days off to go see Alice. He begged me to come with him. Of course, I couldn't tell him how agonizing it was for me not to go after Julie like a year-old eagle does a lifetime mate. I couldn't do it. Stupid. So stupid. Where, when did I think I was going to find the truth? It was like reading the Bible—everyone has to make their own truth from it. I had to know the truth here, nevertheless, but if I did someone would die. It might be a final truth for all three of us—Julie, Ray and myself.

Our new job would be with Aronda Mining. They had a lease nearby on an underground copper property high in the Sangre de Cristo mountains. It would take several months to properly sample and map the property for preliminary test drilling. If we accepted the offer there was no time to waste, all surface exploration would have to be finished by late fall. That meant concentrated, hard work. No extra trips to town—no playing around.

All the old mine roads from the late 1800s were in terrible shape, which meant we would probably be marooned for the whole winter, but it would not affect our work in the old tunnels. We could work underground no matter how deep the snow.

This mine had—a long time ago—some deadly notoriety. Two of the miners working as prospectors had found some rich float rock way below what was now the main tunnel. The rocks were carefully traced where they had broken loose from the enriched fissure. Over the millennia gravity and weather had scattered a few rocks down the mountainside. They contained high-grade argentite silver with a small by-product of gold. These same men had also found numerous larger floats of copper ore. Evidently they had not found the silver fissure outcrop on the mountain. They had simply started a tunnel into the copper body, figuring the two minerals were associated. In a way, they were right.

Piled on top of the difficulty of raising the money for such a project were the problems of hiring good miners, and hauling all their supplies and equipment in by pack mule to build cabins and out-buildings. The struggle against often wild and dangerous weather for four seasons was enough to test the strongest, not to mention the danger of misfired explosions, cave-ins and pockets of poison air. These were determined men. Dedicated men. There was no way, at that time, the miners could pack even the hand-sorted ore from the mountain and haul it south almost two hundred miles to the nearest smelter, at Socorro, and make it pay. So reasoning showed that it was the silver they hunted. They finally found it in the last cross-cut. The vein had been small, but widened some as they shafted down on it. No doubt they had been able to sell some of this ore and keep exploring.

At the very top of the tunnel, someone discovered that the silver vein appeared to widen. It turned into a large pocket of high-grade. They had worked furiously, swinging picks and shovels, hand drilling and dynamiting the plenitude of riches from the earth. Instead of proving up the length and depth of the ore deposit, they stoped upward creating an ever-widening, dangerous hole. The lust for sudden wealth led them to disaster—as it did so many before and after them, around the world.

They recklessly timbered at odd angles forgetting that gravity worked inside a mountain just as it does outside. Then the mountain mined a hundred tons of dirt and ore for them. It knocked eleven men from the sides of the huge hole in an instant, driving their bodies down into the earlier shaft, smashing them to flattened bits and creating a mass grave all in one second.

The cave-in was of such magnitude that their relatives chose to leave the burial site exactly as the mountain had created it. Greed had once again overwhelmed reason and caution. They had tried to rape the mine, and instead, it had resisted, killing them and part of itself all in an instant.

Geologists and mining engineers cannot afford to dwell on such hideous folly. The distraction of doing so can also leave them open to dangerous mistakes. I don't know about Ray, but I could not totally free my mind of these poor souls forever a part of the mountain any more than I could forget Julie's tilted smile.

Ray said, "Well, the money sounds good, but God-a-Friday, man, all winter without seeing Alice. I don't know.

T.C., we're young, and women, especially Alice, are too precious to do without."

"Just meet them in your dreams, old buddy." I said, feeling silly for having said it. "The time will go quickly."

"Well, I don't know about that. You know, well . . . I guess you don't know," he corrected himself, "that I'm really getting pretty serious about Alice. T.C. this is the first time I've ever felt this way. We may go ahead and marry before we had planned."

I said, faster than speed, "Don't worry, partner, there's always somebody, maybe several, to keep the lovely lady company while you're gone."

He looked at me hard then burst out laughing. "You son of a dirty dog. You sure know how to make a guy feel secure."

Then I covered, "Hey, if the winter holds off, we can jeep into town a couple of times to save your sanity and your . . . your romance."

"Well, what about yours?"

"My what?" I asked.

"Your own sanity?"

"Ah, hell, Ray, I did a lot of goofing up until I found the right one. I'll never find it again."

"T.C. that's old-fashioned bullshit. If you lose one you're crazy about, just look till you find a replacement."

"I'm comforted to know that, Ray. Thank you so very, very much." Had he missed the reminder of Julie and the sarcasm? Maybe my best friend was immune to such little blunted barbs—or maybe he was putting me on. As I've said before, the easiest person to fool is yourself.

Anyway, we accepted the offer from Arondo Mining. The reason, of course, was the large bonus offered for our work to be paid in the early spring. It would finally afford us the funds to open our own geological offices in Albuquerque. We could fulfill that unrelenting dream we had shared since we were in junior high school.

There was a large cabin at the site. It was old and crude. Arondo had set us up with a winter supply of food and all the map paper, compasses, tools, ore sample bags and other equipment and living necessities we would need. The company had put me in charge of the operation. I felt proud of their confidence. I suppose it did me good to be above Ray—although at the moment, I did not consciously think about it that way.

It was beautiful country, covered with aspen, pine and spruce-covered country. Wild game—bear, elk, deer, turkey and grouse—was everywhere and watered at the spring below our cabin. In our little spare time we did chores and made the cabin as comfortable as possible. We even put up some curtains my mom was throwing away.

The small mining company that had dug the tunnel and built the log cabin back in 1900 had done a fine job on both considering the tools of the time. The cabin had two main rooms which still had seven bunk beds. They were only slightly private because of a large archway built between them.

There was a third room about ten feet wide and thirty feet long. It was made for critical purposes. In it was a large bin for firewood, which was already filled with cut piñon, and a bin of coal to stoke the fire while we were working away from the cabin. The walls were lined with shelves for all foodstuffs and supplies. The real topper was the strong door at the end. It opened onto a rare jewel: an indoor/outdoor crapper. Arondo had supplied us with everything—even three large sacks of lime to sprinkle on the waste in the unusual toilet. Not a particle of scent ever came through the tight fitting door.

There were four barrels of water with taps at the bottom. If we used it up there would be plenty of snow to melt in case the nearby spring froze over—which it was bound to do. There was a no. 4 zinc wash tub that would be fine for washing clothes and body. A four burner wood cookstove had a tank on the side that would heat our water as we cooked. The stove was also used to heat the cabin. We could have a pot of coffee and a kettle of stew ready and waiting most of the time. Not bad for a couple of young, ambitious mining men who would have an entire page to add to their resumes by spring. The cabin was soon as winter-ready as we could make it. We went to work on the real stuff—Mother Earth and her jealously hoarded treasures. Yes, even she was often plagued with jealousy and just like humans could react destructively.

The surface copper deposit was not hard to trace. Copper showed blue and green where the ore had oxidized and formed carbonates from the millions of years of changing weather. Of course, the combination of oxidized colors were the same tint as Julie's eyes. No matter how I struggled to forget reminders kept slapping me. One barren area was over seventy feet wide. After digging below the surface a ways the carbonates and oxides turned to the chalcopyrite— a sulfide ore almost as yellow as a sunflower. In spots we found the heavy metallic bornite, colored like a rainbow and called peacock ore by the old-time prospectors. Although it would be a long time until we had the final assay results, Ray and I both agreed the deposit had promise.

Anyway, what mineral lover would not desire working with copper? Next to iron it is the most practical mineral on earth. The pure copper sulfides were the first mineral that humans used to make tools and weapons. The modern world would break down overnight if all copper objects suddenly disappeared. Trains, planes, autos, electricity and all it powers—phones, radar, weapons, garden tools and countless other items that hold this particular civilization together—would fail. There would be no more brass rails at fancy bars or bronze sculptures in galleries because copper makes these objects possible. Copper had my respect all right, and I intended to give it respect in return.

High on Mongrel Mountain the aspens were turning the color of the chalcopyrite. They capped the mountain like a great crown of connected golden necklaces. Little white fluffs of clouds had begun to gather every day now, then blow away. Then the first freeze came. The golden aspen leaves turned gray-brown and started softly dropping to the forest floor. The clouds built darker and meatier. We worked side by side with urgency.

Two days before the first serious storm of winter, we completed mapping and sampling all the surface ore that was free from overburden. We had also laid out, spotted and mapped holes for a drilling program. The first steps were complete. It practically cinched our partnership firm of Morris and Young, Consulting Engineerss. I mentally added the word "International" to the logo.

The storm was wild. It whipped down the draws in freezing gusts and piled up the icy white snow in drifts higher than one could reach. When I stepped outside the next morning after the first tempest, I had to push hard to break the drifts free from the cabin door.

It was a new world we now viewed. White, with profound stillness. The limbs of the spruce trees bent heavy under the snow burden. The road—or actually the old trail—that wound its steep way down Mongrel Mountain, was no longer visible. The Jeep we had expected to drive to town was buried in the snow.

The mouth of the major tunnel was the only dark thing visible. Its single eye brazenly looked back at us. It beckoned darkly, seductively, seeming to say "Come and view my treasures. Come and pave the way to my destruction for I would rather be blown to bits by your powder than crumble and die alone over ceaseless time." It would take us a day or so to shovel a path to it.

At first the cabin had seemed comfortably airtight. Then I started feeling little fleeting touches of very cold air. I checked the windows, the doors, even the storage room, but there was no evidence of a fissure in the cabin. However, before I could completely forget the tiny drafts, they would come again across my neck and shoulders, soft as the removing of a silk scarf, just as they always had when I visited the ancient Anasazi sites. Even though I couldn't find an explanation for this different coldness— one I had never felt or been aware of before—I never mentioned it to Ray. I suppose that was the one subject we had never discussed.

It snowed every few days. The soft stuff piled deeper between the frozen drifts. Then new drifts formed on top of old ones. Yet, the strange currents of wind would cover and uncover little open spaces between rocks and the scattered timber overnight. So, everyday it was a different world. Nothing on this vast, undulating, living land was stable, including ourselves.

Anyway, we set to work in the deep tunnel, over a thousand feet inside the heart of the mountain with several crosscut tunnels up to four hundred feet, and shafts and drifts of dimensions and content as yet unknown. We marveled at the determination of the old-timers who had dug this with their crude hand tools. The vein had a general strike northeast and southwest. It dipped to the southeast. It was mostly in a porphyry and gneiss formation. Good rock for a large deposit of copper. The tunnel was a fantasy of colors that belied the deadliness of the millions of tons of earth hanging above us. The colors glowed softly in the flickering light of our carbide lamps. Where we chipped away the air-and-water-exposed surface, it gleamed like a Pharaoh's treasured tomb, and it was just as silent.

Of course, Ray and I had both stopped at the opening of the killer cross-cut to look at the large wooden crosses—one on each side with RIP crudely hand carved in them. We just looked wordlessly and moved on past in the same manner. I was aware that neither one of us even glanced to that side of the main tunnel. We walked on by as if it didn't exist. Then I noticed how the airspace right in front of the opening was several degrees colder than the rest of the tunnel. I started to question Ray about this, but for some reason held back.

Then one day Ray really surprised me. He stopped in front of the cross-cut and said, "You know, T.C., we should go in there and say a prayer out of respect."

"Well . . ." was all I got out before following him in.

The rock was seamed solid enough for safety around us with the same mixture of copper ore as the main tunnel. I thought I heard whispers and looked back over my shoulder. It will sound odd to some, I suppose, but I swear I felt a breeze made up of chilling, invisible whispers. Sometimes I could hear sounds that came almost to the point where I could understand a word once in awhile—

sometimes in Italian, Spanish or some Slavic language, but mostly in English. I strained mightily, but could not get a single word for sure, much less the full sentences that were being whispered for me. Me alone.

About a hundred and twenty or thirty feet inside, the tunnel was blocked solid with the rocks of varying size from the cave-in. There was no hole there for an airshaft. I somehow imagined the soft sounds of frigid, moving air.

Our lights revealed three-inch boards crisscrossed by eleven one-inch boards that were nailed on them. The names of each crushed miner and the varied dates of birth and the same day of death were carved under every name.

We both stood a moment in front of the mighty tomb. Then Ray ducked his head and took off his helmet, holding it in front of him with the carbon lights upright. The beams caused eerie, moving shadows. I did the same, glancing sideways at Ray, who was mumbling a prayer. All I heard was ". . . justified, found not guilty, and made righteous just as if I had never sinned." Then he added, "Lord, bless these fine souls and assure them we are their friends. Amen."

"Amen." I said, that being the full extent of my own personal prayer. However, as we walked out, Ray leading again, I was damn sure certain that I felt a clammy touch caressing my neck and shoulder blades telling me something from such an unreachable place I could not absorb the slightest awareness of the meaning. There was a suggestion of something colder. Colder than death.

Stepping into and down the main tunnel was a relief such as one lost in a blizzard must feel at the sight of the clouds breaking apart and the sun shining through to spotlight a rescue party. Our voices sounded hollow and misplaced in the tunnel depths.

Even in its dark silence the tunnel was almost better than being in the cabin. The snow was higher than our heads along the skinny path between the tunnel and the cabin door. The windows were sometimes covered solid by drifts blocking out the daylight and making the cabin itself seem like a cave. Often the unfathomable winds would clear all the windows and let light in everywhere. Sometimes, a day or night of eerily talking wind would leave a single window clear and open to the fluctuating light.

We had not realized our work would go as fast as it did and that spare time would crush at us with nothing to do but go over and over our reports. Foolishly, the one thing we had forgotten was reading material . . . entertaining reading material. All we had were manuals and mineral books.

At first we talked for many hours about our plans for the future, plans for our new company. We rehashed our youthful adventures, but we never mentioned Julie. That had to wear on the both of us like sandpaper on pine. Eventually our talk became repetitious and boring, and finally we worked, almost silently, speaking only when necessary.

During one of these intermittent discussions, Ray abruptly rose, walked to the window. It was as dark outside as the inside of a locked safe. He spoke aloud, startling me somehow. There was a madness about him, an unpredictable imbalance, yet he intoned soft as a southern preacher who is just finished raising his congregation's blood pressure fifty points and now is in the process of silkily dropping them back to normal—back to the time of collection.

"Old mountain, your language is different from mine, but I hear you. I feel your mighty energy through the darkness. Do not concern yourself with the frailties of our pitiful flesh. We mean you no harm, as we mean none to one another."

This last was almost a whisper, but I strained and I heard. None of it was meant for the mountain. The crazy words were all meant for me. I had to defend myself. So, I grabbed pencil and paper and wrote, speaking each word as I put them down.

"Love and hatred. Love and hatred." Oh, how I thrilled as I repeated these meaningful words that I believed would become his wounds.

"Love and hatred. The eternal contest. Sometimes engaged with swords of the soul. Sometimes with machine guns of the mind. Sometimes with the artillery of delicious deceit. Often, briefly, companions of the boudoir, but finally and forever, love and hatred are in endless conflict."

I went on making thoughtless designs on the paper. When I looked up, I saw Ray still stood motionless at the window looking into the blackness, but now, his broad shoulders and strong back seemed somehow to have shrunk.

I dropped the pencil and went to my part of the cabin and stared out another window, my window, the same as Ray was doing. I saw clearer than summer noon the both of us walking across the red hills of New Mexico, looking for rocks, visiting the ancients (and I was even hearing them) looking for our future. We moved with alacrity and joy. Then I saw Julie sitting beside me that day on the rim of the Rio Grande Gorge. I saw again the sky above all the Taos expanse. It was a sky-bed only God could sleep in. The beautiful sadness was upon me. The night winds broke the silence in long sobs that spoke of infinity. I cried.

I slept little after the first two months, just lying in my bunk, listening to the tossing of my partner and the endless hymns of the wind.

Seventeen

We did have a deck of cards that somehow found its way into one of our survey bags. For awhile we had fun and some relief by the kerosene lamp playing hearts, gin, pitch and other games we had enjoyed so much with our families and buddies during our school years.

I had long ago invented a game called Honor Poker. Actually, it was simply five-card stud with a few changes. First, the player could name the hole card himself instead of showing it. This was to be *honored* as true. The catch: twice in a session any other player was allowed to ask the winner to flip his card over. Ray and I, in all these years, had never asked one another to reveal the hole card— although a number of our buddies had. We played with kitchen matches as dollars or hundred dollar bills according to how high we allowed our imaginations to gamble.

We must have passed two or three weeks of down time with the cards before we started playing Honor Poker. Once we started, we just stayed with it. It was becoming a game within a game.

One night as I was shuffling the deck, the wind was in turmoil trying to tell us something we did not—could not—know. I started talking in conjunction with the wind, not having the slightest idea where the thoughts came from as I shuffled the last hand of the night.

"Do flamingos know they are beautiful?" "Do tigers know they are deadly killers?" I dealt the hole card. "Do snakes know they are cold-blooded?" I dealt the second card. "Do skunks know they are the main ingredient of seductive perfume?" I dealt a third card. "Do eagles know they are majestic in flight?" I dealt a fourth card. "Do earth worms know they are the favorite food of robins?" I dealt the fifth card. "Do the dead know they are dead?"

Ray was looking at his hole card. He bet a handful of matches on nothing but a pair of eights and an ace of diamonds showing. He said, "Do humans know they are the only earthly creatures that ask questions?"

I laughed in silliness and called his daring bet saying, "Surely you don't have the legendary dead man's hand of aces and eights?"

I felt he grinned a little too evilly when he said, "I do, old friend. I sure do." He was giggling as he raked in the pile of valuable matches.

The greatest gust of wind we had heard and felt so far shook the cabin and rattled everything in it including me. As Ray gathered his hand up, I said, "Let me see it."

"See what?" he asked.

"Your hole card."

He looked at me then with an expression I had never noticed before and could not understand.

"You mean . . . you mean, T.C., ole boy, you don't take my cockeyed word? You don't trust me after all we've done together, and all we have left to accomplish . . . together?"

I felt he had talked too long, used too many repetitions, for such a simple request. I swiftly reached and took the five cards from his hands before he could mix and lose them in the deck. I flipped his hole card—the deuce of spades—out alone, in the middle of the table, where we both stared at it.

Then I quietly, slowly, turned over my hole card. It made me a pair of kings to go with my two sixes. I had the winning hand.

I looked at him then, but his eyes were locked on the deuce. This one time at least he was caught and I knew that everything had changed between us forever, and that is a long time.

He looked up with the old enchanting smile I had seen since I could remember and said, "You dirty dog, you caught me in an unintentional mistake."

"I'm so very sorry," I said mockingly.

He took it with a laugh actually saying, with mock anger back at me. "Well, you damn well should be sorry, pulling a dirty trick like that on your old friend."

He had actually begun to believe himself before he was halfway through the sentence. The card game was over. But . . . there would be others. Games, that is.

We went to bed. I did not sleep for a spell because of the little passing-the-time card game and the goddamned house-shaking wind.

Then I thought, as if I had been unable to reason the whole of my life until this moment, saying aloud in the moaning darkness, "The dirty son of a bitch. My best friend has been cheating on me our entire lives." I never knew if Ray heard me. He wouldn't have cared anyway. We would never play cards again.

Then I slept, very erratically, for a little while. I dreamed over and over that Ray and I were in a deep woods and I was his game. I ducked. I crawled. I hid. But, no matter what I did, I could not escape the sudden feeling of a projectile striking me. The missile always come from behind. First, it was a poisoned blow dart, then an arrow that exited my shirt front. I thought, *"What a fine arrowhead that is. It surely came from a master craftsman at my beloved White Bluff Ruins."* Then I was awakened for good by a 30-06 bullet smashing from the back of my skull through my now dead brain and on into oblivion.

Ray was extra chipper the next morning. It was his turn to make breakfast, and he had a steaming cup of coffee waiting for me at my place on the table.

Ray said, smiling like a crooked diamond trader, "Hey, pard, how do you want your powdered eggs scrambled this morning?"

"Hard," I said.

"Think I'll take 'em soft—since that's how I feel today."

"Hey, Ray." He turned to face me, and I finished, "You can't borrow yourself out of debt."

He didn't know what I meant then. I knew he never would.

Eighteen

A few days later he said, "You know what? We're really dummies. We don't even have a pinup in this dump. My God, we don't even have a catalogue we can tear a woman's picture out of to make us a pinup. I gotta tell you, T.C., this is gonna run us nuts. I don't think I can stand all winter without some evidence of a woman."

"Well, ol' buddy, you got to." I told him, "We are trapped." I had brought my .22 pump Model 62 Winchester rifle, our only weapon, up with me in case we had an open winter like last year. I figured a careful head shot would get us some venison, but I was soon aware that all the larger game animals, except the hibernating bears, had moved down to the lower elevations for browsing and hunting food. I had noticed the tracks of some mountain squirrels early on, but now they too had disappeared. There were probably a few snow rabbits about, but it didn't seem worth the effort to find out.

Just the same I said, "Well, we could go hunting, but we only have one weapon."

Ray stared at me with eyes suddenly as cold and unreadable as a fresh snowbank.

Nineteen

The work went on in the tunnel and the snow got deeper. It was a mighty weight closing in like the corrugated steel of a giant vise. I finally told Ray to stay in the cabin and work on the maps. I would take care of the tunnel. He seemed to resent this but was voiceless about it.

At least once a month, the terrible pain beneath the scar on my head would rock me like an overdose of rattlesnake venom. Then just before I was aggravated into screaming fits it would go away.

On rare occasions, things seemed to return to normal and we would visit over coffee just as if we were finishing breakfast at our apartments in Socorro and Grants. We would foolishly plan our office location when we set up our own firm which was now practically assured. We would talk over our school days, especially our senior year of college when the girls and the sports and the fun and all the uncompleted, brand new dreams were invigorating us.

We were laughing freely for the first time in several days.

Ray said, "You know what, T.C.?" I looked at him waiting for the answer. He went on, "I'd like to do it all again and double up on the cockeyed mistakes."

"Well . . ." I choked back and then said, "Maybe not all of them."

Ray went right on, not even noticing my unconscious hint at the destruction of my love for Julie. He was his old charming, cunning, conning self. The difference was, most of the time I recognized his guile now, but not always. I had to remind myself that he was a born master.

It was hard to get Ray's actions out of my mind. I deliberately agitated him. I couldn't help my self "What do you think, Ray? How many bombs do you suppose they've made out of the ore that we personally mapped out. Three, four, ten? What do you think?"

"Seemed they could fill a cockeyed football stadium with them from all the work we did at the time."

"Yeah, well, let's say an even dozen, okay?"

"Sure. Okay. What are you getting at?"

"Well, say there were 140 thousand killed at Hiroshima with one small bomb, then the dozen big ones, we helped make, could kill way over ten million people, maybe twenty or thirty million, huh?"

"Good God, T.C. So what if you are right, there is no use thinking about it." He was getting really agitated. "Having all those bombs may *save* billions of people.

"Well, I can't help wondering how big a part we will have had in annihilating the world. Probably . . . it would probably take three hundred big ones maybe five to wipe out all life on this earth. Turn eyeballs to vapor. Genitals, breasts and other tender parts to acid rain drops. All vegetation to ashes and radiated smoke. Bricks to sand and sand to glass."

Ray was now staring at me. His hands were clasped together almost to the bruising point; his eyes bulged and he was having a difficult time getting enough air to breathe. I'd found out what I must. He did want to kill me. No doubt about it. Even so I couldn't help adding, "You know it will happen. It will come to pass. It is simply how and when. Right, Partner?"

"Wow, are you on one. It would be better for everybody if you'd just shut the hell up."

But I didn't shut up. I went on. I couldn't help it. "We already know from Hiroshima and Nagasaki that radiation eats flesh and gnaws on the bones. What do you think about the fate of all these Indians mining? What will the history of their health reveal?"

"Aw, shit, T.C., nobody can predict history. Nobody."

"Everything is a piece of history, Ray."

"Well, you're sure no historian."

"Listen up for a change. I just told you, all of us are responsible for history. No exceptions. Even you, my friend, are a little stain on history.

"Hey, what in hell is the cockeyed difference? Like you say, maybe everybody and everything will go. Then nothing matters. Right? Nothing at all."

I said, "I didn't mean to make you so upset. Hell, we're just having a conversation."

"No. You were doing all the conversing. At least instigating it, you bastard."

"Listen," I said in self defense, "you and I work on mineralized ghosts. Our lives have been given over to the discovery of the unknown, the unseen."

"Of course." He flipped a hand in the air rudely as if to dismiss my part of the discussion.

"Well, then screw it all," I said.

Ray turned square to me, both hands spreading eight fingers and two thumbs on the table top. He gave me a look that would have knocked a rhinoceros flopping. I knew then that he was planning to do me even greater harm than he had already done. He was going to kill me. That is certainly what his eyes and body language expressed with great force. Again, in self defense, I thought of how I might possibly beat him to it.

Then I slowly dismissed the silly thoughts from my mind. It was the wind. That's all. Just the goddamned wind playing tricks with our nerves.

Even so, I pushed a little more. "It's really funny, Ray, after all our planning and our recent good work, that we'll finally be buried and we'll just be known for one little thing."

He looked at me and, after a long pause, said, "Well, what *is* that little thing, genius."

"Easy. It will be carved on our tombstones: *Ray and T.C. Bomb Enhancers.*" I could see his jaw muscles straining as he said,

"Now you listen carefully, old friend, I don't ever intend to hear about the goddamned bomb again as long as I live. You got it?"

"You know the old saying, Ray, 'It's the truth that causes toothache.'" I smiled tenderly upon him.

Then one morning over coffee, for no reason I could ascertain, I said, quoting a favorite biblical saying of my uncle Bill's straight at Ray's forehead, "'If ye have faith as a grain of mustard seed, ye say unto this mountain, 'Remove hence to yonder place; and it shall remove and nothing shall be impossible to you.'"

Ray set his coffee down on the table between us and looked at me like I was a steel door, at least a minute, then spoke, quoting also, "Romans five through nine, 'Justified, found not guilty and made righteous just as if I'd never sinned.'" Then like a bull fighter making the final thrust of steel downward into the heart of the beast, he continued, "Corinthians six, nineteen and twenty, 'my body is my temple for the Holy Spirit, cleansed, sanctified and I am not my own, but belong to Jesus Christ. Heretofore because of this testimony to Satan, he had no place in me and no power over me'"

Wordlessly, I went to my bed and lay staring at the ceiling trying to decipher it all, but the wind shook the cabin so that my mind thankfully blanked black.

On the few days when the low winter sun could glance off the mighty white drifts, its ray turned the clean windows into colored diamonds. Dazzling. The effect in the cabin was an uneasy one of shadows that moved with the sparkling apparition of the windows and created a haunting, lonely loveliness of some other world and time. It somehow hinted of life almost seen, flesh almost touched, loves almost found, then lost, yet hovering about only visible to the inner eye of the mind . . . at first.

In our forced, close confinement by the great snowfall, it was hard for me to understand how Ray's next request came about.

"You know, T.C., there's something in the cross-cut tomb I think you should see."

If we had been free with one another as in our former friendship, I would have asked him what he meant. Instead I felt his ineluctable stare trying to penetrate my skull as I turned silently away.

Two days passed before I entered the cross-cut. I felt as if I were invading a sacred privacy, and was guilty of some sort of terrible trespass. I had brought along my battery light without understanding why.

The small rocks among the big ones on the tunnel floor

seemed to crunch under my boots and make a protesting noise as if I walked across a roomful of eggs ready to hatch. I was doing something offensive and uncivilized.

At last I hesitantly shined my light fully on the wooden name roster. I stared, immobile except for my hand quivering the light. Three of the name boards had been ripped loose on one side and were bent out at about a thirty-degree angle. I untracked. I moved with the light to better read the names. They were: Sergio Cavelli, Antonio Martinez, and Angus McCullogh.

There is no way to explain the cloudiness that overwhelmed my presence. How? Whom? What? Why? I have no idea how long I stared at the carved names. I do not understand why my light, and the hand that held it, seemed to be physically guided to shine upon the mass of rocks from the cave-in; and there I saw an opening perhaps sixteen or eighteen inches in a ragged circumference dug into the right hand corner of the tunnel. Several varied-size rocks were freshly scattered out on the tunnel floor.

I tried with all my will to deny the whispers and the sudden creeping, penetrating cold that came about enveloping my every bodily fluid and fiber. I strained my hearing capacity beyond its true limit. Even though I was querulous—about having actually heard defined words from the sound not unlike the stuttered hissing of a tea kettle—I followed its beckoning blindly.

I crawled with much fear into the new opening, my arms out in front with the light, squirming over abrasive, bruising rocks. At moments the space was so cramped, so stifling, that I felt I would be solidly stuck making it an even dozen entombed here. Oddly, it struck me that the number should have been an even twelve. Neater, more precise, like a well-placed drill bit.

The murmurs of things almost heard, drew me on like the addictive taste for chocolate or an alcoholic's vision of endless glasses of whiskey. Uncontrollable. Then I saw and felt the tiny crawl-hole widen slightly. Then more. It was such a relief that several moments went by wherein I did not care a whit about being able to return, to escape.

Again the hand that held the light moved without my conscious control. Slowly, achingly upward. There it was! The great stope of silver riches . . . of sudden doom. In a corner of the large hole, at an odd angle, one timber still held. I turned on my side holding the light in the space where once the boiling in the center of the earth had dissipated and deposited the silver into fissures and seams of the magnificent mountain. It had been actuated so many millions of years back that it was useless to count. The pocket of silver had waited all those eons for eleven men to infringe on its beauty, its luster, its timeless privacy. Now a twelfth man had been sirened into its holy space.

Suddenly I knew I lay atop the remains—whatever that might be—of the eleven before me. I stared up the moving beam of light, seeing the great chunks of stone hanging loosely above. It came to me that I might cause their further caving and killing if I took a breath too deeply, or blinked an eye too swiftly.

Then I dared to ease the light back down as carefully as one handles nitroglycerin. My eyes held firmly on a rock approximately three by four inches—the size of a turkey egg. I could not help myself. With a free hand, I reached out for it moving slowly as honey from a jar until I grasped it. I reversed the process, pulling it close to my eyes where I tilted the light to it. I could tell by its weight and its lampblack tarnish that it was heavy with silver. The rock throbbed in my palm like a small dynamo. I knew it was the pulse of the mountain I felt. I put it in my pocket and felt the oscillation through my whole body.

The sighs that engulfed me, as well their messages, were all tangled in my brain. When one first pans for gold, the eye can be conned by the yellow iron pyrites and other yellowish minerals into believing they are the real thing. Later, if there is the slightest doubt, then it is not gold.

The cold presence I had felt so often in the cabin, surrounded me at this moment, like a large breath of thousands of soft, but penetrating, frozen needles. In time—just like with gold—one recognizes this special cold instantly without doubt.

At the risk of my last drop of courage evaporating, I moved forward until I could reach a fetal position. Then with great strain and fear, I twisted my body around and started crawling back whence I had come. It was interminable. I stuck. I panicked. I went murky. Momentarily, it came to pass that, I was in a softening limbo, and was sitting up at the edge of the cave-in back in the cross-cut, holding the light in one hand with the silver specimen safely in my pocket. In a reverie, I took my prospector's pick using the butt end and nailed the name-boards back in place.

The trance state continued, as I effortlessly filled the crawl space back solid with the rocks from the tunnel floor. I was enveloped in a tranquility of profound relief. I felt redeemed.

The wrath would envelope me later when I would question why Ray had returned here at all. There would be one of two answers for my mania. Either he had purposely pulled the name boards away and opened the enticing crawl space to spite my mind until it was rancid, or unimaginable forces were at work. Maybe both. Under the most rampant circumstances, the results on me were the same. He knew it. I knew it and I believed now the almost invisible entities that constantly wreathed coldly over my upper body knew it.

Twenty

From that time on, I would feel a cold touch now and then mostly around my neck and face. These peeks into another dimension would come so fast and so delicately that I could see nothing but a glimpse of a shadow—from the outer corners of my eye. When I grabbed something of substance I only felt the coldness as the specters had already escaped my grasp. Then! Then all would drastically change! The clouds would move past like year-long ghosts and create such a chill of aloneness so sad that it was unreachable. They—the night winds—came from far away in the universe with moans of unknown tongues and shrieks around the cabin and the sharp rocks of the mountains, telling of both faraway and nearby hells and the unrelenting cry of stranded souls.

During these periods Ray and I seldom spoke except as it related to our work. It seemed like we had already joined The Time of Forever.

Using my pocketknife, I had scraped one end of the silver rock clean of tarnish. I worked it smooth and shiny like the finest newly polished dinnerware. I walked up to Ray while he was busy with some maps and silently held it out to him.

He tried to ignore it, but one glance had him. He stood

up and took it in his hands turning it around admiring it greatly. After all, minerals were the only sure love of which he was capable. Suddenly he dropped it on the table, rubbing his hands together and sat back down. His writing hand trembled as he faked his work.

Without a word I picked up the rock and took it back to its place by my bunk. I was enormously pleased. I knew he had felt the life in the rock. I was also sad. Not just for Ray, but the for the multitudes in the world who miss out on such wonders because they simply fear their existence. What a loss. An inexcusable one.

Right after that, Ray began another ritual that would eventually stab at my guts like nothing else. Every day or so he would take a stack of twelve envelopes, nine blue, three pink, out of the crude little night stand next to his lower bunk and read all of the blue letters after he put the three pink ones back in the drawer. He read them slowly, sometimes smiling and once in awhile chuckling out loud at Alice Farney's written words.

I knew there were nine blue ones and three pink ones because I counted them every time he took them out of the drawer. I also knew the nine were from Alice because I had taken him a cup of coffee and got close enough to see her name in the corner of the envelope. I tried to see the pink ones, but never could get close enough before he had stuck them securely away from my view.

My curiosity was unbounded, but I managed to keep my hands off them out of some strange code of honor. I suppose the fond remembrances of the friendship of our youth, when we really were partners, stopped me.

Then one night the coal-oil lamp had been placed just so and the light from the wavering flame moved revealingly across the pink letters. It flashed in front of my eyes and seared my mind. I saw again the three pink letters from Julie that I had burned, along with our love. Oh, so long ago. The son of a bitch had gotten three love letters from Julie and did not even have the decency to read them. What a scummy bastard my best friend had turned out to be.

I chewed on bile until the wind moaned me into an exhausted sleep. The vision had been as painful as ten suns scorching my insides. My head felt crucified and my heart throbbed in ceaseless pain. Anger. Relentless.

A day or so later, I suddenly, uncontrollably sang, "Wonder who's kissing her now, Wonder who's buying Alice the wine." Paraphrasing the song.

Ray raced for the wood box and hurled a fourteen-inch chunk of firewood at my head. I ducked just enough so that the missile barely scraped a bit of blood to the surface of my forehead. It still stunned the thought out of me.

Before I could get to the rifle, he was already dragging me to the wash basin, cleaning my head and apologizing as fast as he could.

"T.C., I'm sorry. It wasn't you I was hitting. It was my own dumb, cowardly self. The cockeyed howling wind just got to me. It'll never happen again. I swear to you with all my heart. My God, we're best friends. We've always been best friends. We always will be. Please forgive me, T.C."

Unbelievably I said, "Hey, it's okay. Forget it. I've been having some of those strange thoughts myself."

We shook hands and hugged. I felt our lifetime friendship come momentarily to my insides, but there was still a hurting, infected vacancy there as well, and I said, smiling in some form of fabricated happiness. "You, my old friend, are a mercury-tongued chicken shit."

He just looked at me with a queasy smile, struggling to swallow.

Suddenly. At that very moment, I decided I would start making preparations for a grand wake for this deserving man.

I ordered Ray to work in the house while I would go in the mine to prepare some more cuts for assaying and later mapping. The one thing I did not want to miss, was the comfort of the tunnel. I felt more at home there alone inside the mountain than anywhere else on earth. I did relish the rare occasion in the cabin when the sun broke through to give us rainbow essences of dancing color on the frozen windows, but at the same time I was relieved to escape, even momentarily, the icy, never-quite-seen fingers on my face that now permanently inhabited the cave-in and the cabin. Maybe they had always been there, but I just hadn't noticed. Funny about things you fail to notice.

I took a battery light into the tunnel to enjoy, even more, the rampant coloration of the mine's minerals. It gave warmth to my soul. A hundred feet inside there was total silence except for a rare, falling gravel that would ding on my helmet. The mountain's warning to be careful of a rock fall became a warm conversation to me.

Once I had met an old prospector in a Magdalena, New Mexico, bar and shared a few beers with him, I remembered him saying, "No need to worry in the tunnels, son, a five-pound rock will kill you just as dead as a whole mountain."

This tunnel was close to 9,000 feet in elevation, so there was over three thousand feet of rock above this level. There were uncounted millions of tons of rock over my head and I welcomed the load. I loved for the old mountain to drop a few little rock-words on my helmet. The occasional pinging pebble is what finally gave me the idea of conclusion with Ray. I remembered that every time Ray finished cutting a sample, he would take off his helmet, hold it out even to keep the carbide light going properly, and wipe at his hair and brow. He was not aware that he did it. I was. So, I cleverly worked some five to ten pound rocks in selected overhead spots so that gravity, or the jarring of a pick striking the wall, would have a chance to dislodge them. I mapped them in my head very carefully, so that I would always be out from under them. Finally I had it all set. With yellow paint, I had x-marked the special locations for him to work.

Ray was pleased when I invited him to rejoin me back in the tunnel. I could tell he felt truly forgiven.

I was so thrilled at my cunning, I marched on ahead and forgot my mind map. I swung the prospector's pick excitedly into the wall, and that is all I knew for a spell. Then I saw the light and thought I had died, but it was not the white one we are told about. It was yellow and flickering.

Ray was holding my head up, talking, "T.C. Young, you are one lucky sucker. That rock must have weighed twenty pounds. Looks like it just hit the back of your helmet and maybe your shoulder blade. Can you stand up?"

With his help, I could. Sure enough where he rubbed his hand across my back was a great welt and swelling. I didn't get much work done for several days. The strong liniment Ray rubbed on my back every few hours might just as well have been shot directly into my liver with a twelve gage shotgun. The smell of it left me gagging as it penetrated into my blood and worked its way into my mouth and it put the excruciating pain back into my overly abused head.

Ray went on working alone in the tunnel and made

all the x-marked cuts, quartered and bagged the samples and located them on the assay map without a single one of those killing rocks doing its plotted duty.

As soon as I felt like it, I went out and with the sharp end of my pick jerked every one of those double-crossing rocks down and hauled them out in one of our wheelbarrows. I scattered them in the snow like a mad dog's slobber. I didn't know if I could ever love that tunnel as much again. I had asked one last special favor of it and it had completely ignored my request.

The winter seemed to reach a point of static despondency as if nature herself had given up the mammoth struggle of changing the seasons. I caught myself fancying a winter without end. A solid season of white until all vegetation vanished and consequently so did all the animals of the world that depended on it for seclusion from man and for the food of life. What would happen to the world? To us? When would our earlier uranium discoveries be processed to make bombs and blow us to burnt dust? When?

Ray continued his silent torture of my entire being by reading his nine blue letters several times a day now. When he would place Julie's three back in the drawer, he always gave me a glance so swiftly I could hardly catch it. There was such gloating in that fleeting look that once I had to go outside and throw up in the snow.

In Ray's restless sleep he repeated the names of many of his conquests. Then one morning at perhaps five o'clock—I think it was about five o'clock because we had long since ceased to wind our clock, since real time did not exist. Nothing was there but the white, white world.

I heard him say, "Julie. Oh, Julie. Please listen to me."

My God almighty! The evil bastard was dreaming of his conquest of my love. Mine.

After breakfast I got my equipment ready to go to the tunnel. In the open door I turned back to Ray and said, "You are such a son of a bitch you would embarrass a rattlesnake."

I could hear him yelling vile things at me after I slammed the door.

The next month passed as it exists on the calendar but for us it was eons of time seeming to be in reverse. We spoke to each other less and less and when we did it was with a spitting growl like two newly caged bobcats.

One morning I took a prospector's pick and prized two loose boards from the floor. I don't think that I was fully conscious of what I was doing at the time. More like a farmer pulling the tits of his milk cow with his mind on a poker game in town. Subconsciously I suppose, I remembered Ray's complaining about the lack of pinup girls.

I took a hatchet and chopped on the boards in various places. Ray stared at me, watching every move but not saying anything. I shaped the boards in my crude way as much like a woman as I could. The legs. The arms. The small head. Then I ripped one of my mother's old sheer curtains from the window and cut it into pieces and tacked on a very short skirt and bra.

When I finished, Ray was standing there tense, his nostrils flaring in and out. I started to say one thing but said another, "Well she's not Rita Hayworth or Betty Grable, but she'll do."

As the winter froze on, the pinup became mine. All mine. I stared at the transparent cloth on the board. I talked to her. Silently, of course. Soon she seemed to talk back. Once I dreamed that flesh had grown under the cloth replacing the wood and she really became Rita Hayworth, the actress.

Ray never spoke to me at all now. In fact, he never looked at me but on past to my pinup board where it leaned against the wall by my bunk. It had not been enough for him to seduce my Julie, now he wanted to steal Rita. I knew he was going to kill me to get her for himself alone. It was obvious.

That night I conjured up a dream. I held the silver specimen from the mountain's main artery, for help. It was a vision really, because I pinched myself very hard on the cheek and forearm to be sure I was having what the old-timers called a "waking dream." The bruises on my face and arm proved the next day that it was a true vision.

She came in a kaleidoscope of movement and colors, her hair gleaming in the sun for an enticing instant; her smile of delight at anything new and interesting to her; her delicate walk of fleshly rhythm that excited me so. It was wonderful. It was terrible. I could not reach out far enough to touch her, but I could smell her special scent. Hers alone. Then she walked away into a huge misty forest and vanished. I lay awake the entire night trying to will her back. My Julie was gone. Again.

While Ray slept, I got up and went to the tunnel. I used my carbide lamp, but carried the large battery light as well. I walked through the entire length of the tunnel as fast as I could and right up to the face of ore where the old-timers had finally quit digging. I shined the bright light on the stunningly varied colors of copper and said, "Ah, old mountain, show me your visions." I waited. My hands were shaking the light now where it made little gleaming moves against the ore body owned by the mountain. We were trying to steal her secret hidden treasure just as Ray was after my new woman. I suddenly felt exhausted. As the dust settled, I sat down and leaned back against the face of the tunnel. I dozed and dreamed vividly.

A larger than usual pebble fell on my helmet. It was heavy enough that it made a thud instead of a ping. I could feel it had jarred my brain almost to dizziness. I did not care.

I yelled, "Please. Please, old mountain."

Then I heard a noise of grating rock. A whole cluster of small rocks fell and there was a momentary gust of dust. Then I saw a great ocean as blue as the finest azurite copper. There was a bubbling spot that rapidly grew bigger and the fiery orange color that only magma can mix came boiling up to the surface. In a few moments of time the inner earth formed a large island. It cooled solid and was swiftly covered with all sorts of vegetation luxuriously green like choice malachite copper and a long, smooth but empty, beach formed.

With a start I woke up and envisioned the beginning of a new continent for no reason I could comprehend. Everything felt incomplete. I remained still. Somehow both expectant and relaxed. Then I surely must have dozed off again.

Now I was walking up out of clear, blue seawater onto the beach. I could not see myself but I could see where I was going as I moved away from the sound of the birds into the jungle of trees and plants. The song of the birds, and their varied mating calls, vibrated pleasantly in the air. There were flowers I had never seen before, and colors I never knew existed. They were of such brilliant beauty and size that they befogged the eyes and the voluptuous scents intoxicated the brain. I was back on the foliaged island.

Then I saw a movement. I followed, but it stayed the same distance ahead of me. When I stopped. It stopped.

Then I caught a glimpse of iridescent hair in a sunbeam between two trees. It was Julie's hair. I followed in exultation beyond imagining. I moved. I stopped. I saw. There was a peek of her naked breast through a circular opening in the leaves. There was a teasing look at her buttocks dancing away, then a flash of her thighs, and her graceful feet keeping her just out of my full sight and my lusting hands. I was out of breath now. I stopped to get it back.

I saw the upper half of her face and bits of her nakedness facing me unmoving. In her eyes, which seemed to move away from her body toward me—just as they had that day across the street from the bank in Albuquerque and the gallery in Taos—was that same inscrutable, hypnotic look from eternities away. Unfathomable.

Then the sea, the island and Julie were all gone. The tunnel was so silent I thought my ears would explode from want of sound. The mountain, or my dream, or both, had cut me off at the moment of my resurrection.

As I slowly walked past the cave-in drift portal, I felt the cutting coldness as always; and felt the suddenly tender touches around my head, neck and ears. Lately I could make out single words in the whispers. Nothing in solved sequence, however. But today I didn't need to connect the words. The thoughts themselves came as clearly as a dry martini. They were complete—these thoughts. At last.

I weighed them carefully as I exited the tunnel. I turned back to the cave smiling as I stood. My soul was giving thanks. I was still smiling until I entered the cabin. Ah! But now I knew what to do.

One day when I came from my tunnel, Ray was down in the floor tearing up boards. He didn't look up.

Ray was never the engineer I was, and he wasn't as

good a carpenter either. His boards were nailed together all crooked, and he had even torn the curtain when he tacked it on. Besides that, he had worked so desperately and crudely that his pinup woman had splinters all over. Some while later I could hear him in the night talking aloud to her.

I was hardly sleeping at all now. I kept trying to have another true vision of Julie. It came without announcement. The pinup board had now completed its metamorphosis from Rita to Julie. I bent a finger back until I almost screamed in pain to be sure this vision was real. It was.

Julie slowly dropped her skirt revealing the perfect legs that moved her body in such enticing rhythms. She easily removed her bra and rubbed her breasts a second in their freedom. She stepped out of her panties as gracefully as a ballet dancer. She turned fully towards me, leisurely gliding forward. My God! How swiftly my breathing increased and the lust of love permeated my loins. I reached out with both arms and hands and she came into them and everything fit. Everything. It was as tender and warm as fluid. I was lost with Julie in that region of the delicious vacuum.

Then Ray had a coughing spell destroying the vision and she was Rita again , leaning against the wall. She had put the curtain cloth back on. I thought seriously about leaping up and choking Ray into silence forever.

Then came the naked beauty of a cloudless day during a full moon. The world around us turned to brilliant baubles from the sun on the undulating snow. That night secret stars came out to bathe in the sweet clearness. Stunning.

Suddenly, I sat up in my bunk enjoying this rarest of soothing sights. Contentedly I dropped off to sleep dreaming of my Julie's body as she bathed it to sleekness. Then I awoke. The blue stream of light came in from another angle now. A new night. I saw that one edge of the illumination was uneven. I rubbed at and concentrated my sleepy eyes. A figure was standing there cut in half by the moon rays. My body was petrified wood. I was hypnotized like a field mouse looking into the merciless eyes of a snake. Sixty five million miles away the sun cast its burning orange rays to the far distant moon where they changed to blue-green as they reflected through all that space to shine in the window of our cabin outlining one half of the apparition standing before me.

I was certain Ray Morris stood there looking at me. Motionless. It seemed he wasn't breathing and did not need to. I did desperately, but couldn't. The scar on my head pained terribly. There was a moment when my entire body turned to stone. Only my heart fluttered wildly, struggling to live. Had Ray altered to stone as well? I could see a rounded powerful shoulder above his upper arms dropping to his muscled forearms where his hands hung curled like an orangutan's. His wide neck held his skull up above all that power absolutely immobile. I could now feel his seething eyes through the moonlight. They sighted along invisible shafts colder than the deepest snow bank on the mountain. Colder than the burial chamber in the tunnel.

I wished and strained so hard, I must have broken some bones. I wanted to leap up and run through the wall cascading down the mountain to my freedom or doom. At the same time I craved the ability to rise and attack, crushing and stomping the still figure of the night to dust and then sweeping it outside so the winds would scatter it about forever. I could not move. He just stood there staring for minutes of years shooting glacial slivers into me. I felt like I was buried in the exact dead center of the Arctic ice cap.

What did he want? When would he come for me? Was it really Ray? Now it seemed it might be a materialized entity from the tunnel. I had not yet moved on the suggestion of the now understood whispers. Had they sent an emissary to bring me to join the eleven others under the great cave-in? I strained to move, to utter a single sound. I was trapped like an unborn baby. I was like a calf being birthed by a mother eland on the Serengeti plains as the hunting leader of a pride of lions stood waiting, salivating.

Then he, or it, moved slowly towards me causing the moon rays to fluctuate as the now clear outline of a man, a ghost, an organism advanced upon me as slowly and deliberately as a giant snail. I lived eternities as I waited its eventual arrival. At last it blocked out the blessed light of the moon and I saw only darkness. I closed my eyes and waited for the blow that would make the darkness permanent. Fear beyond thought was all that was left for me.

I must have lived on in this vacuity for a long spell. It was the trembling of my entire body rattling the bunk against the wall that finally made me aware I still lived. I felt about myself. I could find no recognizable physical injuries. Both the darkness of the night and the moon rays that had temporarily given relief were gone. The violet dawn was bringing life back again. I gave thanks mutely.

The last time I would ever see Ray reading the love letters, I felt the icy fingers touch my cheeks. I whirled with all the speed I could muster to grab at the floating shadow. I missed as always and fell against the wall. As anyone would do, I looked around to see if he was laughing. He wasn't. He just leaned back in his bunk holding a blue page out staring over it with eyes that were as hard and heartless as the blade of a Viking's battle axe—and just as deadly. I could tell his mind was made up now. I had to watch every fearful second until I could reach a final decision of my own.

I puzzled why I suddenly wondered about the color of jealousy. It was no more green, as expounded, than a ripe lemon. It was red as fresh blood and often as eye-burning white as a welding arc at full heat. It also carried invisible knives that stabbed endlessly at the heart and stomach and heavy hammers that pounded at the skull and all its contents. It also made one just plain silly.

I went to bed and placed the .22 rifle under the covers by my side. I sat up and stared at the archway between the rooms until it fluctuated in and out like a bellows. Finally I heard the deep breathing of Ray sleeping.

My mind floated around aimlessly and soon there was Julie's head coming into view, then her breasts, then her waist. She was climbing up marble steps about four feet wide with balustrades on each side. She wore a blazing white dress. Her face was painted the same color. A white cloth of the same material as the dress completely engulfing her hair as her body completed the climb to a level, white-tiled floor. There was just her whiteness against a cloudless blue sky—no, there was one tiny soft cloud.

Now all I could see of her face were her red, red lips complimenting her blue-green eyes. She took three sinuous steps towards me and stopped as I held my aching arms out to her. She looked at me a moment expressionless. She shook her head as if in confused sorrow, blew me a slow kiss, turned and walked to the marble stairway and slowly stepped down again disappearing completely. There was only the sky left now with the tiny cloud, then that was gone as well.

Twenty-one

I almost got motionless whiplash trying to keep from staring into the brain of my ex-friend. It didn't work. He felt it and looked up. To say our eyes locked in combat would only enhance a cliché, but they did just the same. He looked back down at the assay maps he was checking out.

I got up from the chair and went over to get a box of .22 shells off a shelf. I secured the little pump Winchester where it leaned in a corner. I sat right back down in the same position, pulled the magazine out from under the dark blue barrel and methodically started dropping shells into the loading slot. Each shell made a slight, satisfying click as it fell into position. When it was full, I raised the rifle and pumped a shell into the chamber. I pulled the hammer back a tad in the safety position.

Ray raised his head at this and took a quick glance around. I could tell he was a little frightened, but even more puzzled. I liked that.

I went to my part of the house. I put on heavy outdoor clothing—gloves and an ear-flop cap, both were fur lined. I headed for the door.

Ray spoke to my back, "Mind telling me what you're doing?"

"Not at all, friend. I'm gonna kill us a snow rabbit for supper. I have a craving for fresh meat. It's the first day of spring."

"What're you talking about, T.C.? It's probably six more weeks before the bears will even come out of hibernation."

"I'm not after bears. The snow rabbits are coming out today," I said, and closed the door on the warm air behind me. It was about noon, I figured by the sun that was seasonally low in the southwest.

As I struggled up and over a snow bank at the end of our shoveled area, the frigid air shocked my lungs. For a moment I felt very foolish. In a short time of angling through the shallowest parts of the almost solid snow, I had pumped blood through my body fast enough to give out enough energy heat so that my breath was strongly fogging a cloud in front of my face.

I stopped a moment looking for any trace of snow rabbit tracks in the unbroken whiteness. My eyes wandered on across the mighty chastely-clothed mountains and through the tops of spruce far below. I could see on and on. The dark patches of trees only emphasized the massive bulk of stone beneath the frozen white. For a moment I imagined the sun was sending messages to the mountains to just shrug their multiple shoulders and all the snow would break apart and come avalanching down and down creating an instant springtime. The thundering of the avalanches would awaken the bears. They would all exit their winter havens and take a deep yawn. They might rare up and do a celebratory dance for the birthing of the new season.

However, my fancy returned to frozen reality when I looked up above me where the tree line vanished. Up there was only barren, sun-sparkled, white with not a single, frozen flake melting all the way to the intensely blue skyline. As I looked, everything became bigger and more formidable. Unconquerable. So I turned my gaze back downward to a little winding area where the winter gales had blown it almost snow-free. There I saw a snow rabbit digging in the shallow spot to get at a bite of vegetation.

I instinctively raised the rifle to what should have been the proper level, but the actuality of this creature living, breathing with soft fur covering actual edible meat, threw me off. I had to lower the gun to re-sight properly. As I did, the rabbit leaped up a couple of yards atop a mound of rounded snow. It posed there with eyes wide, nose twitching, ears up, every nerve ready to spring its body away to live another afternoon.

The front bead of the rifle barrel settled into the back V and I moved the rifle up in an instant so all centered on the eye. I pulled the trigger. I knew I had meat before the next shell was pumped into the chamber.

The shot had been so perfect and death so instant, that the snow rabbit fell to its stomach and slid just about a foot down the side of the mound. It had only kicked twice. Slowly.

I was almost—for some reason beyond my reason—instantly out of breath. I had to sit down. The rabbit blended with the white so perfectly that only a slight shadow revealed it at all. For a moment I lost its location and thought it had been a temporary vision. Panic. Slowly, my eyes moved and found it again just as the sun moved between two closely angled peaks in the far distance towards Taos pueblo. Its wondrous beams caught a million snow banks that included the one that supported the dead rabbit.

For a magic instant, the world turned to white diamonds and the rabbit was stretched out on one that glittered beyond the capability of the human eye to surround. I looked at the rabbit in all the glorious sparkles encompassing it. There was a bright red trail from its eye, down its muzzle, that curved out on the icy snow like a red comma. The rabbit in its splendiferous setting cried a tiny red river.

Who was the tear for? I wondered. Me? Julie? Ray?

The world? The universe? All I knew was that the rabbit did not seem to weep blood for itself. It was glowingly indelible in its design.

Then the mountain peak hid the sun. All became ivory shadow. I shuddered and stiffly struggled to my feet. I was stiff, but my breath had returned. I felt strong as I worked my way across the indention to the snow rabbit.

I tried to backtrack to the cabin but due to the frozen snow under some of the drifts, I kept getting off trail. Dusk had arrived and I still wasn't sure how near the cabin was. I had another moment of panic—which are rare for me. I had always handled the elements well, but I felt I might be lost. A night of frozen air was rising and shrouding me like a thousand-foot ghost as the sun took refuge from this part of the mountainous earth.

Yes, I was lost.

I lay down on a true, slippery slope and went blank. I think I said a silent prayer. I'm not sure. To know you are lost in a vast, frozen wilderness does things to the mind, to the deepest reaches of the soul, that are unimaginable, unspeakable. I was lost in uncountable ways.

My thoughts went to my Julie and what I was certain I had finally heard from the spirits of the mountain. I was ready to walk myself to death or find my way back to the cabin. There were things incomplete. Things that had to be done so I would not have to come this way again. That is the way it was. That is the way it is. It had always been so.

I stuffed the still-warm rabbit inside my shirt, closed my eyes, taking a slow, but deep frigid breath and started walking, climbing, falling, sliding. I swore I would move until the light of the cabin was revealed to me. No matter what. I stumbled over an arched piece of a fallen tree and fell facedown. It jarred me close to senselessness because the wind had blown the area on the other side of the log almost clear and I had fallen into the frozen shroud of dirt the mountain was attired in. I strained dizzily upright, finally managing to sit on the log. Nothing was broken as far as I could tell. I was grateful. I thought a moment. No. I struggled to think for a moment. I knew that there were countless precipes hidden here. Anyone of them could tilt me over or plunge me downward into a mess of broken, even pulverized, flesh and bones. There were canyons on this frozen mountain so deep that I could walk into and freeze to death before I ever hit the bottom. It was not the best place for an educated, ambitious young man to be. However, if I sat here thinking about it for very long, that is where my bones would be found—if they ever were.

I moved again carefully feeling my way, holding the barrel of the gun and using its wooden stock as a probe. The wind kept me company sometimes in twisting gusts that almost turned me around and it took all the strength my legs contained to stay upright. There was no color to the world now. It was made up of gray-black dampness. The ground, the air I breathed, the entire upper atmosphere was the same frozen nothingness. Nevertheless, I moved.

My eyes had now lost the ability to discern anything at all. I ran into trees. I fell over snow-hidden bushes, but I held onto the rifle. Twice I was sure, I had felt out into space with its stock and turned away from oblivion.

Now though, my heart could no longer get enough of the frozen air through my lungs to fuel my body. I was slowing. Then I was barely moving. I ran into a tree. It hardly jarred me, I was moving so slowly.

So, this was how my odds turned. My short rope of

life had almost been uncoiled. How much was left? It was a question that hung like sacks of rocks from my mind. I didn't care so much. I just needed another few days. Would I get them? Reason could only answer in the negatives. I felt almost nothing now. I saw even less with my eyes and my mind had numbed equally with my lungs. It was about over. *I was going easily* was the last thought I had before I tripped over the fallen tree again. This time it had done me a great favor. Smacking the hard ground quaked me awake, and I became angry at my helplessness.

I felt my way up to sit in the same spot that seemed eons away now. But . . . but my brain worked again. I walked a small circle in the area near the tree. There was the lifesaving log itself, a few yards on a ragged ribbon of a barren rock and then on around some snow-buried bushes. I could keep moving in the one small circle, feeling my way with my legs. I could walk that true circle of life until dawn would give sight back to my eyes. I could do it. I would live and fulfill my little purpose here on earth at this time in this dimension.

Purpose. That was the only word that mattered now. I walked and I walked, endlessly I walked in that circle. I knew, also, that I had to keep my mind working as well as my legs, so I decided to attempt calling up a vision. It is funny about true visions—sometimes you can call them up and then no matter how hard you try, they only come on their own terms. Now both concepts seemed to work as I walked in the visual nothingness.

I mused. This was no spot for a materialist.

At that instant, I felt the dead weight of the gun. Stupid. I leaned it up against the log. Without this added weight I almost bounced along—for about a minute. Soon, so very soon, the feet became leaden again. So, I decided to dance a circular waltz. Of course, my little rutted trail would not allow any other kind. Anyway, I became creative by skipping a step now and then. I also did a little jig, round and round, that is impossible to describe. You just had to be there.

I imagined Julie was dancing with me, but she was doing the leading. Under the circumstances that was just as well because I was not capable of action that measured much beyond helpless.

I'll be a horn-billed, well-driller if the vision I had asked for didn't materialize at the exact right moment. It was way back . . . back in the "Before Time" ten's of thousands of years ago, and Julie and I were mates. We had very dark skin. She carried our child, draped across her breasts and belly, in a lion hide sling.

There was a conference of our small migrating tribe about the need for dried meat and leather pouches of water before we entered the desert that was dry, deadly and huge.

I now stalked the great antelope. I was young and strong, but I trailed him for two days without any intake of sustenance. I was almost within spear-throwing range. The great sword-horned antelope nibbled at a few leaves on a bush and looked around, ears working, eyes staring, nostrils searching the air for evidence.

Oh, if I could only get two more body lengths closer, I had a good chance of hurling the cactus sharp spear into flesh. The antelope heard me thinking. I had to risk it all right here in this instant. There would be no other for us. I unbent in great leaps of adrenaline power right through the bushes and grass and hurled the spear with all my strength sending a guidance prayer down its shaft. The spear heard my prayer as it sailed through space and into the heart of the antelope as he, too late, gathered his muscles to flee. However, his intended action carried him three long strides before he fell. The slick shaft of the spear projecting up like an erection.

It was done. We dried the meat in thin strips for easy carrying. We made water pouches from the hide, and we crossed the great desert to a long green river that split it. We started a new little part of the world that our children's children built into pyramids and golden statues. None of it would have been possible without the antelope giving us his body, and Julie nursing our baby to survive and start the breeding of a new civilization.

Then later, I was with Julie in the land of frozen oceans. I, and my partners, hunted whales and seals while Julie, my lovely Julie, made a comfortable home in our house of ice. We had warm clothes she made from seal hides, as well as, wolves and foxes. She also made us a fine warm, bed of these same animals. We stored the gift of their meat in another house of ice to feast on daily. We had lots of fun in the fur beds. Maybe too much for we were soon working half our life away helping our offspring to build new ice houses and showing them how to hunt the furry swimmers and runners. No matter what—I remember the fun part the best.

All of a wondrous sudden, we were back on the tropical island where I had witnessed the volcano under the ocean give it birth. I was still pursuing Julie's nakedness through the lush jungle of huge flowers and fruit. In truth I had been the pursued. She came up behind me jumping on my back and knocking me into the leaves. She rolled me over face up. She mounted me with her legs spread across my crotch. As I looked up between her pink, pointed breasts she smiled down at me saying, "I have chosen you. You are my husband."

So, there was nothing to do but marry this vision right then and there. The wedding ceremony was celebrated three days later with much singing, much dancing and much drinking of fermented fruits, as well as, the eating of young pigs. Julie stayed beautiful most of her life, because we didn't have to labor much. Everything was growing wild that anyone could ever need. We celebrated our marriage on the forest floor in the leaves just like when she had first captured me. We had much fun in the leaves, until I got so old she had to lift me up afterwards. Finally she couldn't do that chore either. So, we sat around our grass hut and smiled a lot even after our teeth were gone and our bones ached like an arrow in the ribs.

An enormous blast of piercing, driving, murderous wind tried to blow my true visions away. Although the mighty gusts knocked me whirling up against the log, I refused to give in.

On the 2nd of December, 1805, Austerlitz was a small village, but we had 70,000 Russians coming to our aid. It only increased the number to be slaughtered. I was charging in the Prussian Calvary against Napoleon's left flank at the Battle of Austerlitz. There was lots of blood spurting and seeping that day. He had led us into a trap by making our commander believe his flank had folded. Then the Frenchmen came up over the hills on two sides and slaughtered most of us. I was miraculously able to ride my horse away from the last of that coagulating carnage even though I had a sword blade go all the way through my right thigh before I had cut the French captain's head off with one powerful swipe.

In the little Prussian village where I was hidden and nursed, Julie had done most of the healing. She was so caring, so lovely, so special that I asked her to burn my uniform to hide my identity. When I got well we were wedded and bedded. I became an accepted son of the village and worked hard to farm turnips, potatoes and apples. We were fruitful people and lived long lives with love—mixed with a few disasters. We are both buried side by side in the same cemetery as her parents, other relatives and seven of our own children, thirty-four grand and great grand children. It finally took an entire, additional, turnip field to bury us all. Fruitful, I said.

I stared away from my true vision and back to the now moment. There was no dawn even peeking much less breaking yet. There was only the same gray-black horror of immeasurable sameness without delineation. Naturally I turned back to the kaleidoscope of the lives Julie and I had shared together. In one of them. I think it was in Greece. I had murdered Julie by pushing her into the ocean from a rock bluff of great height. In St. Petersburg, Russia, she had stabbed me in the heart from behind. We were both in the service of some sort of great ruler about whom we had obviously had a disagreement. I saw my own funeral and did away with this part of the true vision because I couldn't tolerate my precious Julie crying her blue-green eyes red over my demise by her own hand.

Around the world, we had loved and lived together, my Julie and I. And now I was enormously pleased and enlightened as I looked at the great white bluffs on the San Cristobal ranch south of Santa Fe and Lamy. Here were the ruins where as a boy, I had felt the strongest about the ancients.

Now, they were not ruins. They were strong, connected rock houses, half underground, half above, all through the pueblita. They were clustered around a circular kiva—the worshiping place. A stream that watered the pueblita, the deer, lion, bear and turkeys ran a quarter mile below the village.

I sat making arrows. I was conscious of the need, the survival I gave to my village with these fine points. I had pride. I had position. I was flaking a piece of white flint with a half inch red edge. Then I heard Julie coming— although here and now she was named Morning Song. She held a high position as well. She was the chief herder of the wild turkey flock. She was bringing them in to put in the strong houses and pens made of tree limbs, green, young, so they would bend in a smooth circle and the birds would not injure themselves when the coyote or the bobcat tired to get at them.

Oh, what a beauty she was. She walked smoothly, parts of her rippling like the muscles of a stalking mountain lion. She waved at me and continued conversation with the dimwitted turkeys. She *could* converse with them and no one knew how—not even the turkeys.

I went back to my arrow making. Just the thought of Julie's smell caused me to break the precious white flint in the wrong place. Now there was only enough to make a tiny bird-point, if I was lucky and intensely careful. I was. It came out perfectly under the careful flaking with a piece of deer antler. There it was. My masterpiece. It had a sharp, perfect, red point. I leapt up and stood immobile a second to be sure Julie had penned her flock. She had. I ran fast, shortening the distance by zigzagging between, or up and over the rock houses, to get to her.

"Look!" I yelled, "Look!"

She stopped and waited as I neared. I held out my arrow point in my palm for her to admire just as I had to Ray Morris seven hundred years later.

Her dark eyes glowing with joy at my success, she said, "Yes, it is as beautiful as the bluffs," waving up at the mighty white bluffs towering protectively above and around us. Then she added, "As lovely as the bluffs at sundown." That was the greatest compliment I could ever receive, because our bluffs at sundown are the most beautiful things on the Great Spirit's planet, except, of course, my Julie.

Now, for the really first time, I knew why I loved rocks so much and why Julie was such a natural organizer. I knew, too, the reasons the spirits of the Anasazi talked to us. These current thoughts, away from my true vision, allowed the mountain's mighty breath to breathe on me again. I walked on, in the circle delaying the creeping death for at least a few more moments.

Suddenly I was in Spain as a priest, Father Costa. He was giving the last rites to the merchant/banker, Mercurio Ruiz. With polished and practiced motion I closed the evil little eyes forever. No more would Ruiz look across his great mahogany desk and inquire, with much relish, of the mortgage payments of peons for the eventual foreclosure. No more would his little eyes gleam like black fire opals as he overcharged the poor farmers for wares they could not live without. No more. No more. No more for the little evils of Mercurio Ruiz.

I kept crossing myself as I made my way through the gathering of whimpering relatives. They made moaning sounds of mourning that were as false as a pimp's love; sounds that later in the night of this bright day, would turn to celebratory noises and sighs of vast thankfulness and relief. The master who had cast invisible chains around their necks, making them give their souls and hearts in tithing to him instead of to Father Costa's church, had now left them free—had left them people of property, as well. Now, I, Father Costa, could serve them properly, and they would, in turn, show their appreciation in the warm spirit of good Malaga wine.

Ah, Malaga wine. The Father had only one more stop before he could return to the courtyard behind the church compound and share the late afternoon glasses of the purple enchantment with Julie—Mother Superior.

The Cruz family had been waiting, watching for the

priest's arrival. The door opened before his seventy-year-old hand touched wood.

"Ah, Ernestina, you look so beautiful. Your mother must be improving?"

The twenty year old, unmarried girl smiled in thanks at Father Costa's words, but she knew that she was in fact very plain. So many eligible suitors had finessed their families' wishes in other directions whenever her name was brought up as a possible wife. In Father Costa's opinion, these young men were wrong. Ernestina was a dedicated, diligent and hard working, Catholic girl. She had proven this with the care she was giving her recently widowed mother, Elisa.

On entering the sick room, Father Costa was surprisingly pleased to see Elisa sitting in a rocking chair. A faint smile of greeting crossed her mouth, as her bony, work-worn hands were held out to take those of the priest.

"Now, this is something to see, Elisa, my dear. You are almost well. You will be dancing to gypsy music on the plaza at Seville before winter comes."

"Oh, Father, you give me such hope. I walked with Ernestina to look at the garden this morning. Since her father's death—the affairs of her brothers and their families take all their time—I'm afraid it has become too much of a burden for the poor girl's back."

"Mama, you know better than that. Why, I . . ."

Father Costa shushed her to quietness with his fingers to his lips. With a wink that the mother could not see, he motioned her out of the room. The priest knew that the work was long and tedious for Ernestina, but she was young and good of heart. She also had the strength of the young who cannot depend on beauty and cleverness to get them by.

Turning to the mother, he pulled up a chair facing her. He knew that she was afflicted with the disease-of-loss only. She was healthy as a corn-fed mule, but loss of her husband, had caused her to take to her bed in grief. The priest also knew that the action came from a death wish so she could join him in heaven. But, it was not time. She was not ready. God had other earthly duties for her here. She must be a mentor and spread love through the blood, the genes, the souls of her grandchildren . . . and also, she must see her youngest child safely married.

Father Costa touched her lightly on the temple and smiled great comfort into her watery eyes. "And now for the good news."

Elisa dabbed at her eyes with a handkerchief and opened them wide as if the promised good news would come through her eyes instead of her ears.

"I'm meeting tomorrow at the parish for lunch with Senor Miguel de Martinez to cement a marriage between his fine, hard working, honest son, Sergio, and Ernestina."

A breath of joy and great expectation was drawn into and expelled from Elisa's chest. "Oh, Father, can it be true? Has he given his permission?"

"All I need is your acceptance," he white-lied. Father Costa knew what a good black cigar and a bottle of Malaga wine (named after the nearest great city) along with some talk of deer hunting in the Pyrenees did to Senor Martinez.

His heart was filled as he watched the life force surging back into Elisa's body. She stood up with sudden strength and agility saying, "May I tell Ernestina?"

"Not yet, but do not concern yourself. The Lord has shown me the way."

And such was the daily life of Father Costa.

The priest walked uphill now toward the church standing almost blinding-white as the mid-afternoon sun erased all shadows from its western side. The village, as most Spanish villages, was built and scattered over a carefully selected hill to more easily fight off the many invaders of Spain—the Moors, the Romans, the Carthaginians and more. But now Spain itself had more recently ruled the seas and conquered a great deal of the world. None of that changed the attitude of protectiveness for their villages and farms. It was that domain that Father Costa served.

He made the last upward steps with some stiffness, but legs that still had power. His aging body had held up quite well. Yes, he could make his daily walk to the village for another decade, he was sure.

As he passed through the side gate into the garden of the rectory he felt as if he could jump over a ten-foot fence from a standstill. In an hour it would be time for the five-days-a-week late afternoon ritual with Mother Superior. This rendezvous, this succor was what made possible his ministering to the ill of body, confused of mind, and carelessness with the soul. He was good at it. He acknowledged this only to himself, but he also knew his own sustenance came from the hour and a half with the Mother Superior.

His slightly bent body straightened and his chin lifted at the thought of his after breakfast reading this morning. What a read it had been. Miguel do Unamoto's latest *"Del Sentimiento Tragico de la Vida en Los Hombres y Los Pueblos."* (*"The Tragic Sense of Life in Men and Peoples."*) The book reminded him of some of the tragic passages in the Bible that still uplifted him as he had been all day. Knowing things was what mattered. Cancer struck the kind and the vicious equally. But Father Costa's approach to these victims was always different. However, he felt his visits of consolation were also equally healing. He could hardly wait for Unamoto to finish another volume. He must pass the last one on to Mother Superior.

He always arrived first and watched as his faithful, old servant, Cecilia, placed the black cigar just so on the round table in the courtyard where he and Julie could enjoy the view as the late afternoon sun streaked across the farms and fields below them. Cecilia then poured the Malaga into two crystal wine glasses and set the decantur beside them. No sooner was this done, than Julie, the Mother Superior, came from the nun quarters across the garden. She walked down the sandstone path flanked by small patches of flowers and shrubs. It created the perfect setting.

They sipped their wine with quiet appreciation. He lit his cigar and they visited casually about problems of the parish. She too, was relaxed and comfortable as he spoke of the day's duties, and those yet to come. As she spoke, he heard and appreciated her melodious voice. It was a soft symphony, that with its very sound had comforted him so long. They received nurture for both their beings as their eyes naturally wandered across the landscape. A few hills and parts of hills were spotted with sparse pines that had long ago been both tall and plentiful. Scrub evergreen bushes clung here and there to the rocky slopes like orphans to a new and loving parent. Some of the more nutrient-blessed hillsides were terraced and produced a variety of produce.

Suddenly I was in two worlds at once. Two dimensions

mistakenly melded. I walked in the circle of eternity. The snow was always in my face, chilling my eyes, my lungs, my soul; and yet I watched myself as Father Costa contentedly gazed across his peaceful parish. He stared now, as I did, at a blindfolded mule down below who walked in the same kind of monotonous circle—only the mule turned a large wooden wheel of little buckets. These lifted water from a well which emptied first into a trough for the barnyard animals, then watered the garden of onion, garlic and peppers, as it trickled its way into a tiny stream of liquid life for the small orchard of fig, oranges, and dates.

Around and around we go—the mule and I. The mule in the lowering sun and me facing the growing wind in a darkness that hid the mountains of white. Round and round we went, the two of us. Then the mule faded, so did my other self and my Julie. I was back inhaling the circle of wind.

Oh, how I craved, oh, how I strained to return for just a few more moments of that Spanish warmth. I would gladly lie down and freeze solid as the massive mountain under my feet of granite to share a glass of Malaga with her. And then I had part of my prayer answered. As I walked on just as blindly as the mule, Father Costa and Julie came again for my observation.

The light on the little rectangular orchards came at a lower angle creating a tender aura that enhanced all the senses of sight, hearing and especially smell. The grain fields were turning soft gold now. A team of oxen moved ponderously slow towards a farmhouse. The driver was a black speck in the diffused colors of the late sun. There were sounds now and then, muted somehow to fit the closing of another day; sounds of children's last playtime before barnyard chores, supper and bed; sounds of birds making their last calls of location before the blue-green night came like a blanket slowly drawn over a bed of sleeping children. Then somewhere, closer to the edge of the village itself, music played, every day. As the gold turned to orange, someone played a violin. Father Costa and Mother Superior always smiled at each other, feeling that for some reason the music was just for them.

It was the time of condensed beauty, distilled to its very essence. It was their time.

Father Costa looked at the face he had known so well for so long. How long? Minutes, hundreds of years, thousands of years? It did not matter right now in this moment of immeasurable radiance. The sculptured lines of her face, the strength and warmth of her blue-green eyes and the softness of her mouth that he had loved so long he was afraid to reflect, made him close his eyes as he imprinted the images to memory. As novitiates together, he had craved, yes, lusted after her so deeply that the temptation to gather her hand and lead her far away to a place of marriage and family had almost overcome him. They had both survived those specific temptations and here they were—if not in grace, at least in graciousness. He had, through the years, nights of dreams where he consummated with her and somehow he knew she had with him. If this be a sin then the great Lord must take part of the blame for who really had control—day or night—of their dreams?

Father Costa poured the last of the pitcher of Malaga.

They raised their glasses in a silent salud and smiled. At the first sip of the last glass, their eyes fused quietly contentedly, knowingly, across the ages—their ages together. It was true. It was all.

I walked on in the circle, wanting to return to the warmness of the patio. I moved with stiffening steps around in the circle of cold, the bull ring of the frigid, the coliseum of the frozen. I had separated myself from this last true sequence. I had been both an observer and a participant at the same time. How could that be? For that little matter, how long had I been walking this circle of solitude, this circle that must continue or I would die? If I stopped for one or two minutes, I would be transferred to the land of the dead which in total honesty of observation could be either heaven or hell and in so many varying degrees that all the invented calculators of the world would fall apart trying to make a count. If I gave in for those few seconds, I would surely never regain my lost Julie. I might not anyway.

The possibility of hope lashed me on. On and on. Circling, circling the earth, the galaxy, the universe, all here in this tiny lost spot on the part of the earth I now inhabited. Round and round and round I moved. There was no beginning and there was no end. Sometimes the circle would become a spiral and walk down, down into the earth and then I would start spiraling slowly upward each step an agony eternities long. Timeless. Up. Up. Up into the sky of frozen breath of sameness, nothingness and beyond. I thought, "I am nothing but a merry-go-round of madness and I'm the only rider."

My heart seemed to be frozen solid. My lungs were blocks of ice. My only chance was one last gift of a waking dream, a lifeline from a true vision. I prayed. I begged. I groveled in that endless circle with silent cries to all the powers to the Great Observer. I wanted so desperately to be with my Julie once more, even if it was from the long-ago-time and passed from the present like a single raindrop in a vast desert of sand.

Then it came to me—or I went to it. I know not which and did not care.

We were in a ghetto studio in old Paris. Julie was posing nude for me. I was a true starving painter, but since she had agreed to model for me I had started selling. Now I could eat and buy more paints and canvas and frames. I could occasionally get drunk and celebrate and fornicate. However, that was not yet affordable nearly as often as would have pleased me. I was an artist with a dilemma. Of course, all artists live in permanent dilemmas. It is their juice of life. For the best of them, anyway.

I ached to throw my brushes down, rip my clothes off and hold her to me in the same beauty as she posed, and I painted. If I did, however, I had this great fear that it would take away from her succulent soul that I was, for the first time in a hungry life, able to transfer to canvas. She lived as much in beauty and desire on canvas as she did on the pedestal. Her copper-toned hair and her blue-green eyes both glowed seductively from the canvas as my brushes smoothed her skin in oil paint. I could paint in any kind of dark background. It did not matter. The glow was there. For her body, her totality, brought light and vibrant life to the canvas. She had now become everything to me.

Finally, I had a full showing in a prestigious gallery— of my Julie, and it was a sell out. Julie herself had everyone present almost groveling, and she didn't even notice it. She was such a natural. Afterwards we stole away together and found a little cafe where we could dine, drink and talk. Oh, I was fancily in love all right, and so was she, but we refrained from physical contact.

A week later, I had just asked her to hold her hand out toward me explaining that her gesture must be one that teased. The viewer of the finished product must not be able to decide if she was simply making a careless gesture or one that beckoned. I knew what it was, and I could no longer resist. We were very soon on the old paint-stained, East Indian carpet making our first-ever physical love. It was like a Rembrandt with Julie.

We could hardly keep ourselves apart after that, and we married within a month. We had spent the fortune from my first big show, feeling sure that our love alone would satisfy thirst, hunger and debts. It didn't. Out of destitution, I went back to painting precious Julie day and night. The next show was a failure. We were putting all our life into each other and her poses came off on the canvas flat and almost like cartoons. The printed reviews and competing artists' comments, destroyed me.

Julie took jobs modeling for other artists to keep us alive and somehow managed to buy marble for me to sculpt. I was a natural sculptor and after only ten years of study and struggle, we were rich and famous again. This time permanently. I only do one sculpture a month and

Julie only models for me. I finally did "the beckoning hand" in marble. It was perfect.

Now, in this snow-world as cold and unformed as a block of raw marble, I reached out with one arm hoping to find that beckoning hand again and at the same time I grasped for the .22 rifle barrel with the other. My dead feet were simply being dragged now, and slowly at that. The two disparate worlds meshed for a moment. I smelled the warm air of Napa Valley where we had once arrived over old Route 66. For a brief moment the air seeped down to my feet. Then it was gone, but I saw the sculpture I'd bought on one of our trips from Napa Valley to Paris. I never told Julie that it reminded me very much of her—especially the outstretched hand that offered love, help, kindness, and more.

I almost gave up before I felt a presence in the now blinding night mist. I saw the hand coming out of the shroud toward my outstretched arm. Was it Julie's hand? Yes! I recognized that it was hers for certain. Even here she created light. It was all so simple. I had known her through all time, through every fire, flood, earthquake, plague, war and all the glories of timeless time. Through all of existence. The arm and hand of my forever-love led me over the snow. Its secure, guiding warmth vanished just as I saw the light glow faintly through the thick night air. It was the cabin.

I entered and threw the rabbit carcass on the floor, saying, "See, Ray? I told you it was springtime."

We cooked and ate the rabbit, and for just a little while it was like the ancient craving for freshly killed meat overcame our modern hatreds and deceits. We feasted and forgot for that little bit of blessed time.

Twenty-two

It was March, but the snow was still there, silent, deep like the ice of the Arctic. I had one more day's work in the tunnel. I could hardly wait to finish. My Julie board—Rita had vanished—was waiting for me in the cabin. I needed to talk to her badly. That is when I caught my partner, Ray, caressing my Julie just like he had so long ago. I was motionless. When I let my breath out, I felt the calmest, the most comfortable ecstasy there had ever been. I knew I had to kill the triple-timing bastard. I moved swiftly and jerked the .22 from the corner.

I spoke softly. "Ray." It was the first time I had called his name in weeks.

He turned his head toward me. I shot him in the pupil of his left eye. He fell off the bed onto the floor and was very still. There wasn't much blood, just a tiny, red stream from the eye socket onto his cheek. The small bullet had ricocheted around inside his skull—contained.

I dragged him, face up, outside, but soon realized there was no place to bury him in the frozen-solid ground. I shoveled out a small space and placed him—sitting up—in a snow bank where he would freeze stiff in an hour. Before I covered him with snow, I looked closely at his face expecting a hint of a smile, a grimace of hatred, a tiny scowl of regret. Something. Anything. There was nothing in his expression but the blank mystery of eternity.

A couple of long days afterward, I went out and moved Ray. It wasn't easy. He was frozen in a sitting position as hard as a da Vinci marble statue. I dug and scraped, finally I prized him loose with the shovel. I had no idea what sort of self preservation this action was. I didn't have to actually think about it. All I know is I was driven to hide him somewhere in the tunnel as I had been told by the *whisperers*.

I was calm. I did not understand this comfortable feeling of closure, but I did not question that it was an ordained peace. Ray and I had long been at an impasse as old as bad colds.

I picked up a stick of dynamite, crimped an explosive cap on a very short fuse and inserted it in the proper place to set it off. I carefully wrapped it in a canvas sample bag, tied it with the draw-string, and put it inside my shirt, shifting around to my back. I tightened my belt so my shirt tail would hold it safely in place. I picked up my hard-hat, some matches and a hand light, put on my fur-lined jacket and went outside.

As I passed the chopping block at our woodpile, I picked up an eight-foot-long pole that was leaning, uncut against it. I must say, I don't know why I did this. It is simply proof that I was being helped somehow—guided, if you wish. Instead of the cold whispers I had felt and heard so long, I was now aware of joyous sounds of a warmth around me.

I hooked the light onto my belt and pulled Ray with one arm and the pole with the other. He was really heavy now as the ice clinging to his body added weight. His face looked like it had been the model for an insane painter's portrait. The ice was broken around his head in patterns that made him appear as if he were screaming or laughing at me with a loud silence. I couldn't decide which, as I dragged him awkwardly.

After a long, physical strain, I arrived and entered the crosscut of the eleven spirits. The cold intermingled with the warmth and the voices now. I stopped in front of the wooden list of honored names and turned loose of both Ray and the pole, setting my light on a rock at an angle so that it shined on the carved names. Then I knelt and prayed to the Great Mystery in the Sky who I knew would finally take control of these poor earthbound spirits.

I had no idea why the odd number of eleven had so desperately beseeched me an entire winter to make it an even number of twelve. I was now doing their bidding. I asked the Great Mystery to give me the strength and the wisdom to deliver and accept number twelve among them. Then I prayed with some fervor that he or she would then release them all and let them move on to the next dimension where they would be given new birth and a new assignment of duties according to what they had earned in this place of transition that I presently inhabited.

I prayed and talked directly to the eleven old spirits in an attempt to placate, to soothe, and encourage them to prepare to move on to their separate and eternal destinies. I spoke in the languages I understood—some Spanish, English, and Italian—but I realized this was unfair to the Slavs, the Asians, and the others. So, without any struggle the ancient world language of *Ogam* entered my throat. It had been scattered around the world by voice and rock writings by the Celts long ago. They had conquered the Libyans who were the world's greatest boatmen of the time and spread widely across many continents. Now the eleven entities were excited that we could converse and were all babbling in *Ogam* at the same time.

Finally, I shouted, "Shut up! Shut up! Shut up! Please!

I have permission from the Great Observer to deliver number twelve and free you all from this mountain."

The chattering softened and they were again whispering among themselves finally in pleasing tones. Well, it was about time they gave *me* a little relief. Then I talked above them asking the most powerful to transfer the physical necessities to accomplish the final delivery.

It was no trouble at all for me to remove the rocks that I, myself, had used to block the narrow tunnel-of-cold-spirits. It was as if they were made of cotton candy. I breathed heavier, but my strength was holding up for the more difficult duties before me.

I took Ray and shoved him in the small crawl-way ahead of me until he hung up. Following my guidance, I backed out with much less difficulty that I could imagine, then grabbed the pole and pushed it ahead of me. I felt it hit the hard ice of Ray Morris. I pushed. I mean I pushed hard, with force. I heard a cracking noise as the iced body moved ahead. Then so did I, keeping the pole ahead of me on Ray. As I moved past the spot where the narrow passageway had trapped Ray's body, I felt something as cold as ice. It was.

I took the light from my belt and switched it on. I reached out and touched one of Ray's icy arms and the forearm of the other where they had snapped off. It didn't matter, of course, but it would slow me down some. Now I had three pieces of him to move. At least the arms were light compared to the rest of his body. I proceeded, one part at a time. Tedious for sure, but getting my duty done just the same. The main part of the body hung up again, but I felt a surge of power encompass me because I sensed we were nearing the cave-in and I could feel the eleven entities pulsating under me, adding their strength to mine. I shoved the log hard and felt Ray's body break loose and move out away from the pole. I turned the light on again and crawled along shoving the appendages ahead of me. I almost hung once myself, but knowing I was nearly to my destination gave me the wisdom to pull all my muscles inward, thereby making myself small enough to proceed.

It was almost done. Suddenly my light shined onto the ice-fractured face of Ray Morris as it rolled back toward me. My last powerful push had snapped off his frozen head as his body went into the rock-filled shaft under the stope. I stuck my fingers into the facial indentations and threw it the best I could out into the darkness followed by the arms and the pole. The body parts didn't matter a whit. The spirit soul was what was important and not even an atomic bomb—not even one I helped build—could separate that.

With a great deal of help I had delivered member number twelve. There were no voices now. I suppose, in some manner, I'd forgotten over the eons they were welcoming him home in a dimension beyond my hearing. I knew the rest was up to me. I was on my own again.

I shined the light one last time across the frozen parts out on the rocks. I swear, and I always will, that I saw sharp slivers of ice break off Ray's face as he smiled thankfully at me in forgiving friendship.

I moved the light up and around the tunnel until I finally saw a shelf wide enough to finish my trust. Now, I acquired and unwrapped the stick of dynamite and with my light ready, I set the flame of a match to it. With one hand I held the light on the shelf and with the other I pitched the dynamite up above it. It struck the wall, dropped onto the shelf and rolled to the edge. I could see the fuse sparkling out over the stope. It stayed. I whirled around and slithered out the narrow tunnel faster than I believed possible.

Then there was the explosion and the great falling of loose boulders in the aftermath. This crowded the air out of the space and into the rifle barrel of a tunnel and I was shot out just like a bullet without the spiraled barrel. It was very fortunate that I was mostly through the narrowest part or I would have broken skin and bones of a nature unknown. I was safe and unharmed. Duty done.

Now as a protection to myself, I swiftly, or so it seemed, sealed the crawl space again. I exited the eye of the tunnel out into the fresh world. My world . . . and Julie's.

Later I smoothed the drag marks and dug snow out of the side banks to hide the tracks. I had no fear, no anxiety.

I was just doing my duty like a good engineer as I went on about the job finishing up the maps and reports, being sure all the samples were sorted properly.

The sun shone a little more each day and the clouds thinned above Mongrel Mountain. The snow started to melt and finally the first touch of spring was there. Then almost overnight the snow was melting enough that it went coursing down the canyons in little mad, muddy rivulets. The trail that led downward to the hustling world of commerce slowly began to reveal itself.

It was a peaceful spell with my friend the mountain . . . but, I couldn't let it be . . . could I? I decided it was finally time to take a look at the twelve forbidden letters in Ray's drawer. I went in, carefully removed them, then leaned back to make myself comfortable on Ray's bed. I reversed Ray's actions. I put the nine blue ones back in the drawer and kept the three pink ones. In spite of all the handling I could still smell my precious Julie. A woman's aroma is as unique to a true lover as the most defined fingerprint is to a lawman. I inhaled to the limit of my lungs.

I opened the top letter and started reading. I read it all, but my mind only saw these words:

> *I beg you, Ray. I plead from my knees on the floor that you will tell T.C. the truth. Tell him that you tried to force yourself on me and I fought you off even though it took more strength than I really have. You didn't even apologize, Ray. If you have such little regard for me, at least partially make up for it by telling your best friend the truth. It is your lifetime friendship that has kept me from seeking T.C. out and telling him myself. I love T.C. so much. It has nearly killed me. It is killing me. Tell him before it kills you.*

With numbness of heart and fingers I opened the next one. All it said was: *Please, Ray, confess before it's too late for us all.* I did not think I could handle it, but I did get the last letter open even though I was shaking so I could hardly see the page. There were just two words and her signature: *Have mercy. Julie Goodman.*

Twenty-three

I had shoveled off the porch and worked there with the boards from Ray's amateurish pinup. I finally evened up one of her arms with a hatchet. I nailed it to the wooden leg forming a cross. I was almost certain I heard the low drone of an engine. Then it vanished. I walked out in front of the cabin to get a better listen and stuck the cross into a melting snow bank without thinking.

Yes. There it was—the sound of a jeep engine as it struggled in the mud towards me. Closer. Louder. Unmistakable. I stood sweating in the still, cool, sunlit air and listened to the Jeep grinding in labor.

Then I stared at the cross, standing stark, certain in its meaning. Whatever had possessed me anyway? I grabbed it, pushing the wood hard at the earth as I twisted the arm-crosspiece sideways so that it became a straight looking stick. I tossed it into the slush and stood on it.

The chief geologist of Arondo Mining Company, Den Galbraith, stepped out smiling, coming forward with his hand out to shake mine. He was a blur.

"How did you boys winter, T.C.?"

"Just fine. We got the job done."

"No more than we expected. I guess you guys will be ready for some well-earned playtime. Seemed to me that it was an extra long winter."

"Yes." I said. "Yes, it was."

"Where is Ray?" he asked.

"I don't know for sure."

"What do you mean?"

"He disappeared a few days back."

"What do you mean disappeared?"

"Just what I said. He vanished. *Adiosed.*"

The chief geologist worked his mouth, silently staring at my feet where I stood on the last of Ray's pinup. Finally he said, "Vanished? Well, I'll be darn."

"Yeah. But nothing to be concerned about. He's always wandering off on his own. Even when we were kids exploring Anasazi ruins, I'd look up and he would have vanished somewhere. Always came back, though."

"Well," Den said with a breath of relief. "Let's take a look at what we've got."

I walked up ahead of him and opened the door to the cabin. I showed him the reports including the suggested drilling sites and depths, cost estimates, assay cuts, everything.

Den kept pushing at his glasses as he read, but he took his time and even stopped to make notes about our notes.

"Hell of a winter you boys chose to do this."

"We didn't choose it. Aronda did."

He chuckled slightly and said, "God did." Den had me there. He went on, "These reports look pretty complete at a cursory glance. What else is Ray working on?"

"Oh, you know him, Mr. Perfectionist. He's probably somewhere in the diggings rechecking our cuts."

"Well." "Well" seemed to be the word that settled Den's inquisitive mind. He walked across the kitchen past the rifle leaning in the northwest corner without even glancing at it. He studied the neat stacks of canvas assay bags. Then he turned to me and said, "Looks like about eighteen hundred pounds of cuts to me."

"That's what I'd estimate," I agreed.

"Well, let's see, I'll take about five hundred pounds back with me in the jeep. I don't want to overload on that slick-ass road. When we leave for good, we'll split the load between the two jeeps. All I need is to lose a third of a winter's work over the side of a canyon. Arondo would either fire me or find me a job somewhere in Peru."

"I don't want to have to win a trip that way, but I'd like to go to Peru," I said.

He looked at me sort of expressionless and I decided

against trying to explain my fascination with the ancients of the Americas to him at this time.

We started walking through the mud with the added weight of several canvas bags making us both slide and sink at the same time. There is not a single item of work in the mining world that comes easy. We were also tracking up the floor of the cabin that I had so carefully cleaned after removing my partner.

At last Den said, "Well, that's about all the weight we can risk." Then for some reason he stood by the jeep a moment and slowly looked all around, up the side of the mountain to the top, at the grayish bluffs protruding above like castle turrets. He even stared off into the melting snow banks and the forest below. Then he looked back at the mine tunnel so long the sweat started easing damply out of all my pores.

Abruptly he turned full towards me, pushed his glasses up even though they didn't need it and suddenly smiled as if immensely pleased. He said, "Well, I'll be back in a couple of days to get the rest of the samples, all your reports and your gear. If Ray doesn't return by tonight, you better round him up tomorrow. We got to turn all this work in to Arondo. They are anxious to see the reports. Copper has been down and that's the time to prove up and prepare for the inevitable up cycle, you know?" He emphasized the last two words.

I was about ready to stalk back to the cabin as he leaned over and took a couple of envelopes from the glove compartment, saying, "Shit. I almost forgot this letter."

Sure enough. It was in a blue envelope. I had a hell of a time controlling my breathing.

"You guys would have caved the tunnel in on me if

I'd forgotten these. Miss Farney has been calling headquarters for over a month wanting to know when you guys were coming off this mountain."

"Thanks," I said blankly hoping he didn't see the sweat marks my hand left on the letter. I don't know how, but I could tell that the earth-staring idiot sensed I was lying about Ray just like a coyote can smell a gun in a pickup no matter which way the wind is blowing.

"See you guys day after tomorrow then."

"Everything will be as ready as it's gonna get." I said wanting him to remove his blabbing ass to the hell out of our territory.

Then to my dismay he leaned out yelling. "We better see for sure if your jeep will start."

Of course it wouldn't start. It was as dead as Napoleon.

"Keys are in it." I said as I took the letters into the cabin. By the time I returned he almost had the jumper cables attached. I got in.

He yelled, "Go ahead, give her a try."

For a moment nothing moved before the charge started taking hold. The motor turned over slowly, then faster and it fired. I raced the engine until I was sure it would keep running and signaled him to unhook. By now, I was beginning to despise the bastard's familiar countenance even though he was only doing his job like Ray and I had been doing all the endless winter. I wanted him away from here. I didn't get a decent breath until I could no longer hear the jeep grinding.

I cleaned the mud from the cabin floors before realizing that it would have to be done again the day after tomorrow. One never left a dirty cabin in the wilderness. Someone might need it badly.

I went over to the table and stared down at the hand-delivered letter a long while craving to tear it open, but not touching it. There it was all wrapped up in one little envelope—our loves. Mine and Ray's. And no matter what situation existed, we had left them to work the dark inside of a mountain for months, but then, those elusive minerals were our other love. Would nothing ever change?

I became aware of the uselessness of these thoughts. I got the .22 rifle and ejected the little fired cartridge. I walked outside, bent over and shoved mud up inside the empty shell casing to give it a little weight before I hurled it as far as I could up into the jagged spires. An eagle couldn't find it now.

I went back inside and cleaned the rifle. I got everything ready at a slow deliberate pace, leaving some chores for next day and night. I slept off and on, expecting to hear the wind howl or Ray talking in his sleep. I didn't hear either one. I got everything ready the next day leaving some canned food on the shelves for whomever occupied our home next.

I put the oval silver rock in my survey bag which held my compass and other working instruments. Its feel, its thrumming, had given me much comfort. I slept well the next night. I had done all I could about everything. There was only one great and dreaded chore left—reading the letter. I had saved it for the last morning to help pass the time until Den returned. I stalled, even then.

It was the time. I picked up Ray's letter, the taunting blue envelope, feeling guilty as I tore the end off it. I was invading a privacy. A place I did not belong. I was surprised how steady my hands were considering that I felt as scummy as I would have sneaking about to spy on my grandparents making love. Nevertheless, I read.

My Dearest Ray,

I admire you so much for delaying holding my body. It is truly honorable. However, since you and T.C. went into hibernation, I've had other thoughts and feelings. I've wanted you so very much and I know you feel the same.

I don't think we should torture ourselves waiting for job completions, companies to be formed and all that stuff, to get everything right. Nothing ever gets right, but sharing while you are trying. We both know that . . .

I couldn't read another word. I had committed a great sin reading even a single word. I wanted to ask forgiveness, but I didn't know how. I moved my eyes quickly on through the letters simply scanning it for my woman's name. It wasn't there. I felt numb and empty like a rusted-out bucket. I sealed it back so evenly that it looked exactly as it had when it was delivered.

I placed the violated letter on his work table and wrote a note beside it saying,

"When you get through wandering, you'll have a full day's walk downhill to find us. We all hope you get lost on the way and wind up in Alaska."
Your exhausted friend,
T. C.

Den Gabraith arrived followed by a power wagon containing lawmen from Taos, Deputy Manuel Garcia and Taos County Sheriff, Roland Kent Sanchez. We all made greetings during the introduction, shaking hands.

Den said to me, while looking toward the cabin., "I presume Ray is ready as well?"

I could tell he did not expect Ray to be here. He was too studiedly casual in front of the lawmen.

"No, as a matter of fact, I'm getting a little worried," I said, just as studiedly casual as he was. "I checked the tunnel again right after you left. He is not working there. I have walked circles trying to track where he might have wandered off into the forest, but the snow is melting and running so fast I couldn't find any sign at all. None. And I've been yelling until my throat's raw."

"Well, let's load up. Maybe he'll show up while you boys are doing that. These mountains are big. Been a lot of people lost around here over the centuries."

The lawmen took two large battery lights from the power wagon walked over and disappeared into the tunnel. At one time or the other they had both worked for Molycorp, so they knew their way around mines.

It all came together at about the same time. We were all loaded.

I'd carefully, fondly cleaned the cabin floor last. The officers exited the tunnel temporarily blinded by the early spring sun bouncing off the melting snow.

Sheriff Sanchez said quietly, glancing carelessly around the site, "No sign of Mr. Morris anywhere. No cave-ins. No nothing."

We were all ready to make our final preparations when Sanchez walked over and opened the cabin door. Leaning, but not stepping inside, he almost immediately turned and came back, saying only. "Didn't want to mess up a clean floor like that."

Hellsfire, it was only a gesture. He so very obviously knew Ray wasn't in there.

Sanchez, with the slightest nod, said with extreme politeness, "I'll drive you, Mr. Young, if you'd like. A fellow gets rusty after a long winter away from the wheel."

I tossed my survey bag in the seat and said, "I would surely appreciate that." And I did. Sanchez was one of those ample-bellied men with an even bigger chest. He moved in a velvety way just the same as he talked. He was a person to respect with kindness and a man to be careful around. I knew he was going to smoothly question me about many things while watching intently for a tiny crack to attack. We got in.

Suddenly, casually, Den came over to my side of the jeep and said,

"Oh, T.C. I almost forgot to tell you. Alice Farney met me at the office when I first got back with the samples. She wanted to come back with me . . . but . . . well, you know, I had to talk her out of it. She is waiting for you guys in the Taos Inn." He started to walk away and then said over his shoulder. "I didn't tell her Ray had gone missing. I felt it better you do that."

Shit and shoe polish! Now I had to try and explain my partner's absence to a fine woman and human being, who loved Ray with all her actuality.

I got out of the vehicle intending to talk privately to Mr. Galbraith, but he had already jumped in and started the motor. Deputy Garcia had the power wagon wound up, waiting. I just stood there. Paralyzed. I felt like I had been shot in the butt with a poisoned dart. Helpless and hurting at the same time. I somehow moved and composedly sat back down by the sheriff. He tossed a quick glance and even quicker smile my way, then followed Den's jeep onto the trail of mud.

All three motors droned and growled down the mountain. The vehicles were spread about a hundred yards apart with ours in the middle. Their motors complained like three old toothless male lions who grudgingly had been sent out to hunt by all the females in the pride.

I had caused several of the sheriff's silky questions to glance off. He had been silent a spell waiting. Waiting to sense where the seam was. Then he said with much dignity and a quick sideways glance with his huge brown eyes, "A little later on, Mr. Young, we will have to return to the mountain horseback with the dogs, even though they'll be working on a cold trail by then."

"Very cold," I agreed, wishing I could remain wordless.

"Between us and the lock on the hen house door, Mr. Young, I don't think we're gonna find Mr. Morris before the bears and the buzzards do."

"Exactly what *I've* been afraid of," I said, looking across a deep blue canyon through wisps of graceful moisture forming from the sun's rays on the melting snow.

Sheriff Sanchez broke my reverie with, "You know, Mr. Young, that I've seen sniffer dogs find a body four or five feet deep covered with packed down dirt. You never can tell though, everything's got to be just right for 'em to work well. The moisture in the air, the mood they're in. So many different things enter into a successful body hunt."

I was silent this time, but knew those all-seeing Spanish eyes had taken in my reaction.

Then he laughed as softly as the feathers of a baby chicken and had as a deliberate afterthought, "It . . . just might be . . . on a successful day of sniffing, that the saints themselves decided to bless the dogs. Quien sabe?"

"I suppose the saints have off and on days like the rest of us." I said.

"Sí. Yes, Señor Young," he agreed, relaxing into his native tongue, and this time he laughed out loud and his belly shook, his mighty chest heaved and his large eyes almost squinted shut with his official pleasure.

I suddenly felt the throb of the silver rock from my canvas bag there on the seat between us. I wondered if Sheriff Sanchez felt it as well. I knew he was capable of many things. I wondered on, and decided I had three decisions to make and fulfill as soon as we got to Taos. Number One: Alice Farney's presence there would come first. Looking her right between her lovely, giving eyes would definitely be harder than the other two. Number Two: Oh, my God, what if, as I fully expected, Alice and Julie had become close friends? How, oh how, was I ever going to face the inevitability of discussing both *her* Ray and *my* Julie with her? Third: if I survived that encounter, I would make a will as soon as I could get to an attorney and have the silver specimen buried with me. I felt closer to the rock than anything else right now. We had been through quite a bit together and I would have the best part of the mountain with me as long as there was a world.

I looked ahead and to the right across the misty canyon again. I saw Julie's face. The moving mists distorted it, but there was no mistaking the eyes as they came forward, bigger and bigger. Bigger than the sky. Surrounding all. It was Julie's mountain, too. She had come to me there in the "changed form," and had saved and succored my soul as well as my earthly life from a tomb of snow. Our mountain became irresistible again.

I turned my head back up at the dark tunnel orb that made the mountain a massive Cyclops staring out across the sweep of the universe. It also peered silently inward to the millions of years of secret treasures it held in its arteries and enriched areas right up until this instant.

Sheriff Sanchez drove on silently now, determinedly fighting the wheel of the jeep on the muddy trail-road for the survival of us both. With our erratic, sliding descent, the line of trees covered one edge of the tunnel portal, then half then all of it. It was gone from sight.

I looked ahead again and Julie's eyes dominating her classic face had moved backwards getting smaller and smaller above the immense Rocky Mountain Range. I sought desperately to see what I had sought before they vanished, but they, too, were gone, gone, gone, vanishing into the infinite.

I felt Sheriff Sanchez's eyes cast swiftly at me for a fleeting instant away from the dangerous road. I wondered if he had noticed the celestial smile on my face commingling with the rivulets flowing from each of my weeping eyes just like those coursing down the sides of our mountain. Forevermore.